BROKEN WORLDS

An Anthology
Volume One

Edited by Louise Cole

Contributors:

Gary Bonn

Janet Allison Brown

Gaius Coffey

Louise Cole

Jae Erwin

Girdharry

Steve Godden

T.F. Grant

Alf Haywood

Patrick LeClerc

Shuna Meade

Cath Murphy

C.M. Salter

Bill Sauer

Ren Warom

William Webb Jr

Firedance Books

God Comes Calling, Cupcakes for the Soupman, Entanglements, 4 Walls, Jinty, Chug a Monkey, Vox Vocis, My Father's Micrometer, I Remember, The Ripped Veil, Scorched Earth, The Star Gazer Tribune, Rising Tide, Underworld, Wetback and *Silver Cop* first published in the UK by Firedance Books in 2012.

The Mortician and Mr Grimley originally published online by *Every Day Fiction* in January, 2010.

ISBN: 978-1-909256-11-8

Firedance Books

firedancebooks.com

CONTENTS

ABOUT BROKEN WORLDS

WELCOME TO BROKEN WORLDS, A fractal study of fractured lives, shattered dreams, dysfunction… and how at the farthest edge of despair, humanity can find joy, hope and redemption.

Editing this compilation has been an intriguing and revelatory process. What happens when you challenge fifteen writers from around the globe to share their interpretation of a 'broken world'? They take us on a strange and wondrous journey through techno-futures, divine and diabolical games, heartbreak, murder, madness and regret. But they also show us the depths of insight, compassion, love and faith, which shine brightest in the darkest of places.

These stories span all genres: cyberpunk, literary fiction, thriller, romance, spec-fic, sci-fi and absurdist comedy.

Broken Worlds is our gift to you. We hope you enjoy it.

Firedance Books. Words that burn.

Louise Cole, Editor
Broken Worlds

GOD COMES CALLING

JANET ALLISON BROWN

'WHAT'S FOR DINNER?' SAYS TERRY, shrugging off his donkey jacket. His knee clicks as he sits at the formica-topped table, and he swears and rubs it hard.

'Hurting again?' says Angie, slipping a fried egg on to a pile of chips.

'Aye. Bloody thing.'

'You should get to the doctor then.' She hands him the plate, sits across from him and lights up a cigarette.

'You not eating again?' he says through a mouthful of chips.

'I've got another five pounds to lose. I'm going to smoke myself slim.'

'You look all right to me.'

'Not in my bloody bikini I don't.'

'You've got three months before we go away.'

'I've got two months, twenty days and'—she looks at her watch and inhales deeply—'half an hour if we leave at teatime. Cleethorpes here we come!' She looks over to me and winks.

He laughs. 'Daft cow. Well, leave a bit of lard on those bones. I like something to hang onto.'

She swats at him across the table. 'Crude bugger. The kid's got ears, you know.'

He turns to look at me and quickly looks away. 'Like he understands.'

'He's eighteen. 'Course he understands,' she says. 'Don't you, Mekki?'

And I do, thanks to the cardboard walls in this shit house.

There's a knock at the front door, swiftly followed by two rings of the bell. Neither of them move.

'You going to get that?' asks Terry.

'Nah.'

Terry gets to his feet with a sigh, his knee clicking again. He crosses the hallway—three steps, heavy on the right foot. The door sticks: bottom left-hand corner.

'Yes?' says Terry. 'Can I help you?'

'Can *you* help *me*?' says a voice. A young man's voice.

'What do you want, mate? We don't buy on the doorstep.' Terry is jabbing a finger at the sticker on the bay window; it's a dull thumping sound.

'What *do* I want?' says the young man.

It makes me smile, inside my head. The man's inflections are *funny*. There is silence from the front door and I can picture the scene. Terry isn't renowned for good humour. He'll be taking a threatening step forward right about now. The other man doesn't sound like the type to back off. There could be a stand-off.

I feel a frisson of—something. Excitement? I'm not generally fond of strangers. First they stare with horror, then with pity; then they try to pretend they're not staring; and then they just forget I'm there. I'm the invisible boy.

When I was little, about five or six, Angie decorated me all up with fairy lights and tinsel. It might have been Christmas. I hope it was Christmas. She wrapped the lights around the wheelchair and the rods that approximate my spine. She wrapped the tinsel around my head brace. It itched my face something awful but, of course, I couldn't tell her that. I sent my fury blazing out of my eyes but by then she was already immune to fury—mine, her own, anyone's.

She probably thought the decoration would make me look more approachable, but mothers still crossed the road to avoid us, clutching their kids to their side.

To be fair to Angie, she only tried it that one time. There really isn't much you can do to make my kind of disability look friendly.

And yet, here I am, trapped inside this broken body in a rundown kitchen, slowly dying from passive smoking, one minute suicidal with boredom—not to mention the pain—and the next minute feeling *excited*.

'Who the bloody hell are you?' demands Terry.

'I'm God,' says the man.

There is a beat of silence and then the smash of a slamming door.

'Who was that?' says Angie, exhaling smoke with every syllable. It's not that Angie can't hear; it's that she doesn't listen.

'Jehovah's Witness,' says Terry, slipping into his chair, and swearing as his knee clicks again.

After that, Terry goes out drinking and Angie and I watch the soaps until he comes back. He is, once again, too drunk to carry me to my bed.

'I'm sorry, love,' says Angie, tucking a blanket around my chin and popping a kiss on my forehead. 'He doesn't mean to be unkind.'

She turns out the light and leaves me in the corner, in the dark, upright in my chair with a thin blanket to keep out the chill. The smell of grease lies heavy on the air. I hear her trudging up the stairs. She pauses outside her bedroom door, then turns the handle and steps in.

He's on her the moment she enters the room, as always, and as always she pretends to like it. Christ, he's stupid. Even I can tell she's faking it. She has to time the orgasm right; too quick and she'll have to go a second round. Too long and—well, it's just too bloody long. Get it right and his manhood is served, every which way.

Christ. No son should know these things about his own mother.

There she goes. Spot on; his cry mingles with hers: 'I love you, Ange!' Then he swears, and then he snores. A stupid man at peace.

I hear her get up and start to move around between the bedroom and the bathroom. Then the house falls silent.

I can see the digital clock from here. Seven hours and eighteen minutes until daylight. The fridge hums. I need a fag; I get withdrawal symptoms at night.

* * * *

'Face it, Ange, he won't know any different.'

But she is adamant. 'I won't do it.'

He gets angry. 'I'm bloody sick of it! I sit here day after day watching you wipe up his spit-sick-and-shit. He's a millstone around your bloody neck—and mine! There's not many blokes would put up with it, Angie. Not everyone's like me. Most men wouldn't do for him what I do. I'm just saying.'

Her eyes narrow. 'And what is it you do for him?'

Don't do it, Angie.

He is hurt, outraged. 'What do I do for him? And who the bloody hell carries him up to bed every night? Hauls that bloody wheelchair from here to kingdom come?'

'He spends every other bloody night in the bloody kitchen because you're too bloody drunk to carry him upstairs!' she shouts. 'Most of the time you pretend he's not even here!'

Mum. Don't.

'He should be in a home! He's like a dumb fucking animal. He doesn't know you, you daft bitch! He won't know the difference!' He storms out of the house, slamming the front door.

Angie lights up a cigarette. 'It'll be all right,' she says. 'We'll leave him soon. He's not much use anyway. I'll find someone else. Don't you worry.'

She's talking to herself.

* * * *

At teatime Terry comes home as if nothing has happened. The fact is, as much as he loathes living with me, he loves living with my mum. She takes good care of him. She feeds his appetites—of which he has many, all of them voracious. His definition of happiness is a good meal and a good fuck, preferably three times a day. And he calls me the dumb animal.

There's a knock at the front door, swiftly followed by two rings of the bell. Neither Angie nor Terry makes a move.

'You going to get that?' says Terry.

'Nah.'

Terry gets to his feet with a sigh, his knee clicking. He crosses the hallway—three steps, heavy on the right foot. The door sticks: bottom left-hand corner.

'You again!' says Terry.

'Indeed,' says the young man from last night. He sounds pleased with himself; again, an impulse of excitement runs through me.

'What do you want?' I'm surprised to hear a note of civility in Terry's voice; I wish I could see the man on the doorstep.

'I want to come in,' says the man. 'I want to see Angie and Mekki.'

'You what?' says Terry.

And then, somehow, the young man is standing in the kitchen, beaming at Angie and me. 'Hello!' he says. 'I've been looking forward to seeing you two again.'

'Who are you?' asks Angie. She's smiling. Perhaps it's the sight of Terry's outrage.

'I'm God,' says the man, and he puts out his hand.

'Pleased to meet you, God,' says Angie, and she shakes his hand.

He has very blue eyes but is otherwise completely nondescript. He has an air of childish delight about him, as if everything is thrilling. But there's something more. Terry is an idiot but even he has some basic instincts and has understood that our stranger is not a man to mess with.

'Mekki,' says the man. He looks me straight in the eyes and he takes my hand and shakes it. Then he looks around for a tissue and wipes the spit from my chin. 'What's for tea?'

'You're not staying for tea,' begins Terry.

'Egg and chips,' says Angie.

The man is sitting at the table. He eats tentatively, as if he has forgotten what food tastes like. He catches my eye often. 'What about Mekki?' he asks Angie.

'What about Mekki,' says Terry. He has been astonished into silence. This oaf, my mother's latest boyfriend, who can be turned into a fist-flailing maniac at the slightest provocation, has no idea how to handle the stranger's confidence. The stranger expects to be here, sitting at the table; Terry can find nothing to argue against.

'Mekki's already eaten,' says Angie. 'Terry doesn't like to watch him eat.'

The stranger starts to laugh. 'I don't think Mekki much likes watching Terry eat either.'

My eyes widen; the stranger has lifted that thought straight out of my head.

'Call me God,' says the... says God. I smile inwardly; God smiles back.

Angie puts down her knife and fork. 'God,' she says. 'You mean... *the* God?'

'The one and only.' He smiles at her. He is kind.

'If you're God, I'm the bloody Pope,' says Terry and he laughs.

God looks at him closely. 'No,' he says at last. 'You're not.'

'So what're you doing here then?' says Angie, pouring him another cup of tea. 'I'd have thought you were much too busy running heaven to come down here making house calls.'

God smiles. 'House calls are my speciality.'

'And what do you want, exactly?' says Terry. 'Mister God.'

Terry is not good at sarcasm. Angie grins down into her lap. My eyes are swivelling from one face to another. I am enjoying myself.

God shrugs. 'It's your turn,' he says.

Terry is taken aback. 'My turn? For what?'

God smiles at me.

When dinner is over, Terry wants to go for a drink, but God is showing no sign of leaving. So instead, Terry helps Angie with the dishes. He teases her, and kisses her on the lips several times. He is marking his territory.

God sits quietly at the formica-topped table. When the cleaning is done, he gets to his feet. 'Let's take a walk!' he says. He does not wait for a reply. He pulls my chair out of the corner and easily manoeuvres me into the hallway, into my coat, into the cool evening air.

'Now wait just a bloody minute,' says Terry.

'Ooh lovely, I need a walk,' says Angie.

I breathe in deeply. I haven't been outside since Angie made Terry take me to the corner shop for a packet of fags two and a half weeks ago.

'Cigarettes are bad for you,' says God. 'You should get out every day. We'll go to the park.'

It's twilight, so there is no one to gawp at me. I'm warm inside my coat. The trees are budding and I can hear things rustling in the undergrowth as we pass by.

'Don't you just love the spring?' says God.

Terry snorts. 'Mekki wouldn't know a season from a sledgehammer.'

That's surprisingly...

... 'poetic of you, Terry,' says God.

I'm filled with a sense of wonder. This God person knows I'm in here. We're on the same wavelength.

'Did you ever consider getting Mekki any tools to help him communicate?' God asks Angie.

Angie shrugs. She has never doubted that I'm in here, and that's enough for her. She doesn't need proof, even if she thought that proof were possible.

I, on the other hand, am desperate to have my voice heard, and I know exactly how possible it is. I've seen it on the television: head-control mouse emulators. They use ultrasound or eye movements to control the cursor on a computer. Of course, I've never been able to tell Angie about it.

'Don't worry,' says God, and he tells Angie.

At home, we go on the Internet, and he shows her a clip of a man in a wheelchair just like mine, wearing a headpiece and looking at a computer screen. Words appear on the screen, as if by magic, and an electronic voice reads the words.

'Bollocks,' says Terry. 'Look at that. The lights aren't on because there's no one at home. Don't fall for it, love. It's a gimmick. God's trading on your hope.' He looks across at me. But there is something new in his look. I can almost hear his thoughts: what if the kid isn't a dumb animal after all?

That's right, Terry. Think of all the things I've heard and seen. Every arse scratch, every private fart, every time you've called in sick and gone back to bed; every time you said you'd mind me and then spent the day in the pub. I'm the watcher in the corner. Think on that!

'How much does it cost?' says Angie.

'Like we've got any money,' snorts Terry.

'We've got holiday money,' she tells him.

* * * *

My first coherent words are `fuck off terry`. Angie cries but God laughs. I am very proud. Also a bit dizzy and sick with excitement.

`Animals are nice. I am an animal. I am not dumb.`

Look at that. Punctuation and everything. And they say watching television is bad for you.

'My boy has a voice,' says Angie.

`I hate eggs,` I tell her. `Prefer your hair brown not blonde.`

Terry sits in the background, speechless and horrified, like it's the wheelchair talking. I am almost sorry for him.

`Been here all along,` I tell him. `Ta da!`

* * * *

We become comfortable together, Angie, Terry, God and I. I cannot move, and remain entirely dependent on others. I am in constant, un-relieved pain and always will be. But I have a voice. I can interact. I can agree, or object, or complain. I can tease and laugh and play. I can whine, and I do, quite a lot.

It's not just me that's been re-born. I always knew what a star Angie was. She never gave up on me, never put me in a home, never treated me like a burden or an empty vessel. She's put up with some pretty horrible men over the years, either because they were big and mean enough to lift my wheelchair, or because they were willing to put up with me.

I always knew Angie was a star, but she didn't. Discovering how right her instincts have been—it's given her a whole new confidence. She glows, honestly, she does, like she's finally got something right. She's stopped the whole bleached blonde thing that Terry loves so much, and has gone back to her natural brown. It suits her. She's only thirty-five, and now she looks it. When I hear her now, at night, I can tell it's the real thing. And when she's had enough, she says so. And Terry takes it.

I thought Terry's days were numbered. I thought he'd leave, or she'd kick him out. But her new-found confidence has been a good influence on both of them. He's more careful. He's kinder. I think, maybe, he's always been a nice bloke inside. He just acted up because he could.

We all have a new voice.

God is the one I can't work out. `Why do you stay?` I ask him at last. `Don't you have other worlds to run?`

God looks sad. 'Do you want me to leave?'

`No. Just thought you might be busy.`

'The other worlds are as broken as this one,' he says. 'Heaven too.'

`What does that mean?`

'It means exactly what it sounds like. Nobody believes in anything any more. Everything is broken.'

`I was broken,` I say. `You fixed me.`

God shakes his head. 'You're not fixed.'

Yes I am. I was a broken doll. You saw inside
me. You joined up my inside with my outside.
I am not broken anymore.

'Really?' says God.

Really.

'Hold onto that thought,' he says. 'I know I will.'

He moves out the next day, although Angie tries to persuade him to stay. I am sorry to see him go.

* * * *

Angie is dead. We'd been shopping and she was pushing me home when a boy-racer in a souped-up mini mounted the pavement and hit her. She's a small thing, my mum, but she's strong and she's determined. She pushed me clear before she flew up into the air and landed on the road, breaking her spine.

How stupid. My spine is already broken; why waste a perfectly good one like hers?

I am back in the kitchen. I have been alone for hours. My computer is on but the screen is black. It's all very well having a voice, but pointless if there is no one to hear it.

The funeral was this morning. Afterwards, Terry brought me home and then he left. I don't know if he's coming back. I am trapped. I find myself wishing that mum had put me into a care home. Instead, I will probably die of starvation—if grief and despair don't get me first.

It is one in the morning. I have soiled myself. I am hungry and in pain.

And then—miracle of miracles—there is a sound from the front door. The door sticks, bottom left-hand corner, and then there are three steps in the hallway, heavy on the right foot. I hear a knee clicking.

Terry flicks on the lights. 'I'm sorry, lad,' he says. His voice is thick with alcohol and emotion. 'I forgot the time. I'm so sorry.'

He lifts me gently, carries me upstairs. He cleans me up, gives me a warm bath. When I'm tucked into bed, he goes downstairs and reappears fifteen minutes later with a meal. It's rudimentary, but it does the job. He cradles my head as he feeds me.

'There you go, son. I'm sorry I was so late. I shouldn't have left you like that. I was in the pub having a drink. With God.' He hesitates. 'Do you want to talk?'

I blink twice, our new signal for 'no'. I don't want to talk, but I want to listen.

Terry says, 'Do you know, that clever so-and-so lived with us rent-free for almost three months! We housed him, we fed him—I think your mum even bought him some clothes. And now he's living off some other poor sucker! He's shameless, even for God.'

I smile inwardly; Terry smiles back. Then we both cry.

It will be hard without Angie, without my mum. I love her and I miss her so badly I can hardly bear it. But I am good at bearing things. For now, at least, Terry and I will muddle along. When we both feel better, chances are that we will move on. I will end up in a care home, I know that. I know that, but I don't mind. I lived with Angie for the rest of her life, and that mattered to her. She never had to give up on me. I don't think she would have survived having me in a home. I'm not sure I would have survived, either, then. But I have a voice now, and I am not alone, what with Terry and God who, I suspect, will come calling again some time when I most need him and least expect him.

CUPCAKES FOR THE SOUPMAN

BILL SAUER

WHAT'S COOKIN' SOUPMAN?'

Every morning, Isadore 'Izzy' Donato would ask the same question, followed by a pleased-with-his-own-cleverness snicker.

Every morning, Marty Samuels would smile and endeavor to make his response sound as chipper as could be.

'I've got my beef barley, a nice Italian wedding soup, my signature potato cheddar beer and a new saffron chicken mushroom with quinoa.'

'Ooh, potato beer day, nice. Wait'll I tell the guys. Hope you're makin' a lot.'

'For your crew, Izzy, of course.'

'Sweet. See you at lunchtime, Soupman.'

'Later, Izzy.'

Marty Samuels was a cook. Holding two culinary degrees, he could have gone by the title 'chef.' He preferred 'cook' and would never hesitate to say so. He wanted nothing more than to use his powers to bring joy to everyman, not just an elite, trendy few calling themselves 'foodies'. Everyman, in Marty's thinking, would be more comfortable with a cook than a chef, and smiling, satisfied faces meant more to him than five-star reviews in glossy magazines. That's why he wanted to open a food truck long before the concept exploded as a hot culinary scene. His dear Great Aunt Sophie would have backed him on a restaurant in New York or LA, Chicago or Dallas, anywhere. Instead, he chose the hard sell—peddling gourmet-quality comfort food out of a truck in New Detroit.

Aunt Sophie finally agreed to finance him when he promised to go with a brand new, custom-built vehicle instead of settling for used, and she got to pick the name.

Kartoffelsuppe—potato soup, in her native German.

Marty couldn't be happier. It summed up his philosophy in one beautiful, rhythmic word. He just wished she'd stayed alive long enough for him to pay her back, which he could have done many times over.

'Hi Marty, sorry I'm late.' Danielle, his assistant, had come in through the truck's rear entrance. She turned around and shook out her umbrella. 'Rain's supposed to stop by noon. We're going to be wicked busy, aren't we?'

'Yeah. I already told Izzy it's potato beer day, so they're going to be cold, wet, miserable and looking for a warm-up.'

'I need to chop extra potatoes while you go see Lady, don't I?' Danielle had a knowing smile on her face, the kind a best friend gets when they recognize your ulterior motives better than you.

Danielle had worked with Marty from day one, starting as his first order-taker and making her way up to full assistant. A sassy little redhead with an infectious smile, he'd met her at a local franchise restaurant. He was so impressed by her personality and service skills, he stole her away, paid her well enough to make it through her last three years of college without needing additional loans. The day she graduated with her restaurant management degree, he made her his assistant. By then, it didn't matter what another employer might have offered her to leave him. Her loyalties were locked tight. She'd tell anyone who'd listen that Marty was the big brother she'd never had.

'Hey Danni, hey Marty. Oh my God, what smells so freakin' awesome?' Tanya, Marty's second cook, made her way into the working area of the truck. Raven-haired, olive-skinned, with big, green eyes, she and Marty had dated while both were at culinary school. He'd thought about making a life with her, but a family emergency forced Tanya to drop out of both the relationship and her education. Marty still hired her on the spot the day she finally came to see him. Their mutual attraction continued but remained unspoken, even ignored. Though he knew she had good reason, Marty never quite got past a feeling that she'd abandoned him.

'Is that the saffron chicken?' she continued, all grins and wide eyes.

'With mushrooms and quinoa,' answered Marty. 'We'll call it Tanya's Nom Nom. If it sells, we'll put it on regular rotation.'

'Squee,' she exclaimed, bounding across the floor to wrap her arms around his neck. 'You're the best. Boss. Ever.'

Danielle smiled wide. 'She's right, you are the best. You always give our ideas a chance. Now get going and get the bread. We have prep from here.'

'And say hi to Lady for us,' added Tanya, rolling her eyes as she turned away to begin her work.

* * * *

Marty stepped out into the cold, damp October morning. The weather had transitioned from an actual rain to soaking wet air, so he decided to brave it without an umbrella. As he turned up the collar of his duster he looked to the construction site across the street. The wooden barriers were plastered with a new skin, scores of the same flyer stapled up overnight. A red circle-A symbol stood out from a black background with yellow text, repeated endlessly down the street. Above the barriers, Marty noticed that the steel structure finally resembled more a high-rise office building and less an urban skeleton. Marty's reputation and some long-time customers in the city clerk's office had helped him procure the permits that allowed him to leave his truck exactly where it was for the duration of the project. Three years, they estimated. One had already passed, and business was better than ever. Izzy and his crew loved themselves some hot soup.

Marty pulled his handcart from the truck's underbelly storage bin and started for the street corner. Calls of 'Soupman!' and 'Potato beer day, yeah!' were barely audible above the chaos of diesel engines, rivet guns and steel, but Marty still heard them and waved as he turned north up the next street. With his back to the construction workers he caught one more shout, a sing-songy schoolyard taunt, 'We know where the Soupman's going!'

A variety of small shops lined the street, from a seamstress to a used electronics shop to a vacuum cleaner repairman. Marty's destination sat a block down, between the pawn shop and a small storefront art gallery. *Lady's*, a bakery owned by the mother-daughter team of Mama and Leticia Diogo. No one knew Mama's name. Leticia went by the name 'Lady', an Americanized version of 'Lettie'. As much as *Kartoffelsuppe* carried a reputation as the area's go-to place for lunch, *Lady's* packed them in for morning pastry, donuts and coffee.

Every morning Marty made the block-and-a-half trek to pick up four boxes of warm baguettes from Lady. Every bowl of his soup came with a hand-torn piece of fresh bread. Lady's bread was yin to his soup's yang, he would always say to his customers. He'd repeat it to her, too, just before trying to convince her to join him for dinner. Every morning Lady would smile and politely decline. For two years, they'd flirted every morning. It was no coincidence Marty had fought so hard for his current location when he first caught wind of the construction project a year after meeting her. He could never get enough of her deep green eyes and full lips, and he especially adored her accent.

'One of these days I'm going to win you over, Lady,' said Marty as he stacked boxes onto his cart.

Lady smiled, as she always did, and nodded in the direction of her mother. Marty looked over to Mama, working a batch of dough with her back to them.

'Mama D,' he called. 'Tell me again why I can't marry your daughter?'

Every morning, the same question. Every morning, the same reply. Some muttered Portuguese followed by a dismissive hand wave. Lady would always refuse to interpret. Marty heard rumors around the neighborhood that Mama wanted Lady to marry a rich doctor and no one else would do, or that Lady had an off and on relationship with some rich stockbroker. He remained hopeful anyway, but Mama always finished her reply with some English, to be sure she'd been understood.

'Because my daughter is no fool, Marty Soupman,' she said. Usually, it would end there, sometimes with an added wish for Marty to have a good day. This was an unusual morning; she added, 'But you will have a good day. We are make extra bread for you now. Today will be very busy. You come get it later.'

Marty had no reply this time, beyond 'thank you'.

Lady followed him out of the shop. She never did that.

'I wanted to ask your opinion on something, Marty.'

Again Marty found himself short on coherent sentence production. He'd become pretty certain he'd fallen for this woman. Really, truly, he'd do anything for her if she'd just say yes. He smiled the way a man does when he's trying to hide a melting heart.

'Okay, shoot.'

'Mama wants me to start selling cupcakes. You know, the fancy kind.'

Marty crinkled his nose, his natural reaction when he heard talk of anything he deemed a passing food service fad. He didn't realize he'd done it until Lady's smile faded away. He didn't intend to do it. He didn't want to do it. He wished he hadn't done it.

'Bad idea?'

'No, I'm sorry, no,' stammered Marty. 'It's a good idea. I just naturally scoff at trendy stuff.'

'Like food trucks that are all the rage now?' Lady crossed her arms and shifted her weight to one side.

Marty wanted to run away. No, cry. No, run away, hide and cry. Two years, and he'd blown it in an instant. Of course he'd never admit it. Of course his visible reaction would be the opposite.

'That's not fair,' he said. 'I've had my truck for years, long before the TV food channels noticed them.'

'So, developing my own cupcake identity is bad because I'm late to the party?' Now Lady's eyes held that mix of anger and pleading that terrifies a man to his very soul.

'I didn't say that. I said it's a good idea. You should go with it. You'll be the best ever. I gotta go.'

'Okay, see you later,' said Lady, her voice shrill. She whirled around and darted back into the bakery.

Marty pushed his cart of bread back to the truck with his head hung low.

* * * *

'Detective Timmins just left, Marty,' said Danielle as Marty handed her the first box of bread. 'You know that big, global banking thing happening at the hotel three blocks down?'

'Yeah. Is that today?'

'Yup. So is the big protest.'

'Is that what all those anarchy flyers across the street are about? That's today too?'

'Yup. So he said to expect a lot of police and media business.'

'Okay, call…'

'I sent a text message to Lucas. He has class until eleven but he thinks he can get here by noon if he can find somewhere to park.'

'That's why you're the brains of the outfit,' concluded Marty. 'Send him another message, tell him to go straight to my usual spot. I'll move my car around the block before the street fills up.'

Danielle nodded and began deftly working her thumbs. Marty turned to sprint across the street and Tanya, her hand on one hip, raised an eyebrow. 'How's Lady?'

He waved the back of his hand toward her as he slipped into his car.

* * * *

Lunch broke every sales record Marty had ever set. By one-thirty they were on their third batch of potato soup and Tanya's Nom Nom sold out. Lucas was lost in the crowd, taking orders. Danielle took in money while Tanya handed out the soup as quickly as Marty could fill the bowls.

'Oh crap, we're almost out of bread,' he muttered. Louder, he said, 'Tanya, get Lucas' attention. We need a bread run. Mama D said she'd have more for us.'

'Lady just called,' answered Danielle. 'Mama's on her way here already.'

Marty went back to muttering. 'What the hell is going on today?' Mama D never left the bakery, except to go home at night. Never.

'Yo, Marty! Mama's lookin' for you,' shouted Lucas.

'Get in here and cash,' called Danielle. 'Tanya, switch with Marty while I wash my hands. Marty, she must want to talk to you, so get out there. I'll serve until you get back.'

Like an efficient machine, the team shifted and Marty stepped out of the truck, nearly into the box of baguettes Mama D held in front of her.

'I brought you the extra bread I promised,' she said, her expression tight with anger, her voice low.

'I was going to send Lucas,' he replied. 'You didn't have to walk it here. I do appreciate it, though, thank you.'

'I heard what you said about cupcakes.'

Marty took the box from her, his eyes wide, his mind stumbling over fractured thoughts.

'My daughter's cupcakes are never for you, Mister Marty Smarty Soupman. Have a nice day.'

Mama D turned and walked away. Marty stood motionless.

'Marty.' Barely audible.

'Marty.' Distant, ten feet under water.

'Marty.' The crowd noise returned like an out-of-control train.

'Marty! Get in here and get going!'

Marty shook his entire body like a dog coming in from the cold and went back to work.

* * * *

Dark. Quiet. At least as quiet as a busy city can be, but compared to the barely controlled chaos of the day's business and the din of the construction site, distant traffic noise and the occasional dog bark seemed almost calming. Marty, Tanya and Danielle were the last people left anywhere near *Kartoffelsuppe* at seven forty-five in the evening. They had just finished clean-up and the counting of receipts.

'That's the Pride Parade day's record times three,' said Danielle. 'What the heck.' She started giggling.

'Just an extraordinary day, I guess,' replied Marty, his tone flat, his expression blank; not that anyone could see it, as he had his head down while he filled out a banking slip.

'Why are you so down? We should be celebrating!'

'Yeah,' added Tanya, 'what the hell did Mama D say to you?'

'Nothing important,' answered Marty, chin firmly against chest.

'Maybe it's about time you gave it up,' Tanya replied. She waited until he turned his head to look at her. His eyes held a mix of bewilderment and annoyance. With what Marty knew was her best disarming smile, she continued. 'Seriously, Marty. All those years back, at school? I had to leave, but I sure didn't want to. If you took me home to make me dinner tonight, I'd marry you tomorrow.'

'Tanya!' exclaimed Danielle.

'What? I'm just sayin'. Admit it, you'd give us your blessing.'

Danielle blushed, sporting a bashful grin. 'Yeah, you're right. I'd say do it tonight, if I thought we could find a judge.'

'Stop it, you two,' said Marty, returning his attention to the paperwork.

'I ain't kidding,' said Tanya. 'Any time, you just say the words. I've been watching you bang your head against the great wall of Lady for more than a year, and I'm tired of looking around when the best guy I've ever known is right here.'

'Yeah, what Tanya said,' added Danielle. 'Can I be your Maid of Honor?'

'Hell yeah, girl.'

Marty didn't look up, just kept writing. 'Fine, Tanya, I believe you. I love you guys, too.'

'I'm just saying that Lady doesn't deserve you, is all.' She wrapped her arms around him from the side, hugging tightly. 'And she's got nothing on me.'

'Group hug,' shouted Danielle, joining in from the opposite side.

Marty couldn't hold back his smile. 'Okay, okay, okay. Now get this to the bank. And go together; I don't want either of you carrying this much money alone. Timmins told me he'd send a uniform at seven-thirty to escort you to Danni's car, so he's probably out there waiting.'

Marty received simultaneous kisses on each cheek.

'Come out for drinks with us,' said Danielle as she stepped away. 'We should be celebrating.'

'Yeah, boss. Come get me drunk,' said Tanya, still holding on.

'Tell you what. I'll meet you at Sully's in an hour or so. If you're going to keep me out late, I want to plan tomorrow's menu now.'

They both agreed and stepped out of the truck. Danielle ducked her head back into the entrance. 'Make sure you show up, Marty.'

Marty opened his menu notebook and dove right in. He lost all track of time until the sound of breaking glass from somewhere blocks away pulled him out again. The distant screech of a burglar alarm followed. The clock on the counter read eight-thirty; he was going to be late getting to the bar. He stepped out of the truck to check the padlock on the drop hatch. The police patrolled the block regularly, due to the high-visibility nature of the construction project, the local businesses around the corner, and the simple fact that a lot of police officers were faithful *Kartoffelsuppe* customers. Marty hadn't had a single security issue in the year he'd been parked there, but it had been such an unusual day. He wanted reassurance. Something felt wrong.

He noticed the street opening three blocks south had an eerie orange light to it. A second shattering of glass, a second alarm from the same direction had Marty looking around him. Under a cone of streetlight, the construction barrier caught his eye.

The protests! Something is breaking bad.

A third crash broke his calm; it was followed by rising shouts and more breaking sounds, of wood and metal and more glass. Marty thought he heard a gunshot.

It's coming this way. No time. No time!

Back in the truck, he grabbed a roll of duct tape from the toolbox. Back on the street, he ran across to the barrier as quick as he could. A dull thud sounded from down the block. Smoke rolled out of the same street opening. Marty started snatching flyers off the wall, trying not to tear them. Lucky for him they were stapled, not glued. He saw the head of a crowd emerging from the smoke like a stampede of wild horses.

No time! Oh God, oh God, oh God!

He stepped out of the light, not wanting to be seen.

Coming this way. Oh God, no time. Oh no, Lady!

He took one last look at *Kartoffelsupppe* and sprinted for the corner, trying to tear off pieces of duct tape as he ran, trying not to stumble.

The first shop on the corner, the seamstress. He hastily taped a flyer to her window, another on her door. Next, the insurance man's office. A flyer for his window; skip the door to save time. The shouting changed from a distant rumble to the sound of angry words not quite discernible. Louder, closer. The used paperback bookstore. Marty loved that store. Flyer on the window, one on the door. Same on the vacuum cleaner repair shop. The lights went out in the pawnshop. He thought they must have known what was coming. Flyers for them, then on to *Lady's*. The lights were out, the security gates closed.

Thank heavens they didn't stay late today.

Three flyers on the window, one for their door. The shouting sounded close, almost on top of him. So many angry voices. More glass shattering, the sounds of pounding against metal, more glass, all just around the corner behind him. Marty's eyes became moist. He knew his world was breaking under the feet of an angry mob. He kissed his fingers and pressed them against Lady's door, then moved on to the art gallery. He had one flyer left, for the main window.

A narrow alley ran between the art gallery and the next store, Mr K's electronics shop. A quick glance behind him, and Marty saw the first rioters come around the corner. He slipped into the darkness of the alley and ducked behind a trash dumpster.

Oh God, oh God, oh God, oh God, where are the police?

For the first time, he could make out some of the shouting.

'Naw, leave that one. They're on our side!'

'Screw the insurance guy! Free health care! Smash it!'

The sharp crash of glass followed, and wild hooting and hollering too close for comfort.

'No, don't mess with the bookstore.'

Running feet getting closer. The morning's rain returned as a light, cold drizzle. Marty slid down to sit with his back against the dumpster, tucked into the corner it made with the wall. He hugged his knees and closed his eyes tightly.

'Cool, the bakery's on our side, too! Maybe they'll give us free donuts in the morning!'

Countless feet scurried past the alley. Marty shrank down tighter.

'TVs! Yeah!'

Marty imagined the rain to be glass shattering all over him, the sound of it was so close. Mr K's alarm klaxon went off as though it were right in his head. He pressed his forehead to his knees and waited.

The urge to get away overwhelmed him. He crawled forward to poke his head around the dumpster. Bedlam reigned beneath the streetlamps: men wearing bandanas over their faces were running back and forth, some carrying large objects. He could see a pile of something burning in the middle of the road, flames climbing hungrily. Shivering with cold and fear, soaked in his own terror, Marty snuck deeper into the alley. He climbed over the fence at the opposite end, up a fire escape on the other side. Marty liked to explore the neighborhoods where he parked the truck, so he knew the area well, the back alleys and fire escapes and which rooftops were close enough to jump across. He made his way home in the dark and rain, to the roof of his apartment building. He didn't know how long it took, he only knew how tired he was.

After a hot shower, he opened a cold beer, fell asleep after one sip.

* * * *

A couple of detectives recognized Marty and motioned him past the crime-scene barriers. As he passed, uniformed officers offered condolences: 'Sorry we couldn't stop the bastards, Soupman.'

He rounded the corner and saw the construction site; ten-thirty in the morning and it stood silent. Deserted. He forced himself to look to his right. No evidence of any glass remained on the truck's carcass. No windshield, no headlights, no windows in the doors. For that matter, no driver's side door at all and the passenger door hung barely attached by one hinge. Dents and missing paint everywhere, spray-painted anarchy symbols, all four tires flattened.

At least they didn't burn her.

He hadn't been able to reach Tanya or Danielle earlier in the morning, their cell phones not even going to voicemail. He wished he had. He needed a hug or two.

As he got closer, his sadness turned to frustration. He cursed under his breath, his fingernails digging into his palms. He stuck his head in the back entrance. It stank of urine and vomit and he went no further. The padlock on the drop hatch remained intact. Pounding his fist on the truck and shaking his head, Marty went around the front to the driver's side. On the shredded seat cushion sat two pristine cupcakes.

One cupcake: a red velvet color with a dollop of white frosting holding a red candy heart. The other: dark chocolate brown with a Taijitu on top, the curves of yin and yang flawlessly rendered in black and white frosting. Marty whirled and sprinted around the north corner.

A large crowd had gathered in the street outside *Lady's*. The insurance office had plywood emergency barriers in place of its window and door, any glass and rubbish already cleaned up. The rest of the shops seemed undamaged.

A voice called from the crowd as he approached. 'Marty!' Danielle. She had spotted him first.

A rousing cheer followed. 'SOUPMAN!'

Marty scanned the crowd. Mostly construction workers, firemen and police. He made out Detective Timmins and Izzy, Mr K, Mr Jameson the insurance man and all the rest of the shop owners. Lady and Mama D stood by their door. He didn't see Tanya anywhere.

Danielle ran to him. 'Oh my God, Marty. I'm so glad you're okay,' she cried as she hugged him tightly. He hugged back.

'Define *okay*.'

'Listen, I already talked to our insurance guy. Everything is covered.'

'I'm okay then.'

He put an arm around her shoulder, she an arm around his waist, and they walked to the crowd.

Marty noticed Mr K's store had also been boarded up. No flyers were left on any of the intact stores.

Someone said, 'Soupman, you're a hero, dude.'

Another: 'Quick thinking, Soupman, nice.'

Izzy: 'Hey, good move, buddy!'

Marty couldn't make heads or tails of it. How could anyone know what he'd done?

Lady walked up to him; Danielle stepped away. Still no sign of Tanya. Smiling, Lady took his hands in hers. Marty noticed a shockingly large diamond ring on her left hand.

'Mama and I were working late yesterday, testing cupcake recipes,' she said. 'When the news said what was going on, we locked the doors and turned out the lights. We saw what you did.'

'Really, you were in there?' Marty replied. He couldn't get his mind around the ring. 'You must have been so scared.'

'We were. Mama thought you were being crazy at first. She wanted to go out and yell at you. Then the crowd came and we hid. I called my boyfriend and told him I'd marry him if we got out alive. He asked me a couple of days ago. When it was all over, Mama said I should be sure to thank you.'

Marty smiled, nodded, despite the fact that he wanted to fall over dead on the spot. 'So that's why you left the cupcakes for me, to thank me?'

'What cupcakes?' She let go of his hands. 'What is it with you and my cupcakes?'

Someone in the crowd shouted, 'Soupman,' and an impromptu chant erupted.

'Soupman! Soupman! Soupman!'

Lady moved out of the way as Izzy and a fireman stepped up. The fireman held a helmet full of money.

'We passed the hat, Marty,' said Izzy. Izzy had never used Marty's real name before. 'To help you get a new truck.'

'Soupman! Soupman! Soupman!'

'Guys, guys!' Marty shouted, raising his hands above his head.

Someone shouted, 'Speech!'

'Guys,' Marty continued, 'I'm no hero. I hid in the alley and pissed myself.'

'I would too,' someone else called.

'Ain't no thing,' said another.

'Guys, Danni made sure we had killer insurance. We'll be open again in no time. Mr K, do you have insurance?'

From somewhere in the crowd, Mr K replied. 'Mr Jameson said the company is claiming *force majeure*. He can't even get them to pay for his office.'

'There you go, guys. Mr K and Mr Jameson need the money, not me.'

Behind him, the bakery doorbells jingled, followed by Tanya's hushed voice. 'Thanks, Mama. I couldn't hold it any longer.'

'As a matter of fact,' Marty continued, pulling out his wallet, 'I want to donate too.'

'Martin Rudolph Samuels!'

It was Tanya. A collective 'ooh!' rose up from the crowd.

'I called you a dozen times last night. I called every hospital in the city. I went by your place twice. I stayed up all night baking cupcakes just to keep from freaking out.'

Marty felt her hand on his shoulder, let her spin him around. Before he could respond, her hands held his face, her lips pressed against his. He looked past her, at Mama D standing under the gilded lettering on the bakery door. *Lady's*. He closed his eyes and accepted Tanya's kiss, crushing the wallet in his fist as another 'ooh!' rose from the crowd. Tanya pulled away by just a few inches, gazing at him with her emerald green, sparkling eyes.

'Screw them Marty, look at me.'

Marty saw hope in those eyes, compassion in her face. He wrapped his arms around her and held tightly, squeezing his eyes closed.

After a few moments, he put his hands on her shoulders and found her gaze again. It had always been the eyes. Tanya's eyes.

'Do over?' he whispered.

Tanya raised her eyebrows and cocked her head to one side. 'You sure? I will not be anyone's substitute.'

Marty's face dropped. 'You're not the one who was a substitute.'

'I've been trying to tell you that.' Tanya took his chin in her hand and raised it to face her again. 'My cupcakes are always for you, Marty Soupman.'

He took both her hands and kissed them. Hand in hand, they turned their backs to *Lady's* and addressed the group.

'Guys,' said Marty, 'I hate to do this, but I have an announcement to make. *Kartoffelsuppe* will not be back.'

Hushed silence. Blank faces. Someone uttered 'no way.'

Tanya squeezed his hand. He caught sight of Danielle, nodding.

'It's time for us to move on.'

Entanglements

T. F. Grant

FELIX PADDED ALONG BESIDE ME in his new combat chassis and I smiled at the police officer on guard outside the apartment on the *Broken Queen*. A shipwrecked ocean liner turned into a condo is still an ocean liner, the walls of the corridor still steel behind their wood veneers, the doors still solid and set into metal frames, the carpet, though thick and soft beneath my feet, still laid upon a steel deck.

'Lucius Blake,' I said, 'Chief Inspector Colerain is expecting me.'

'The chief inspector expected you over two hours ago, Mr Blake,' the cop said.

'Is that you, Malcolm?' I asked. 'I can't tell under all that armour.'

Sergeant Malcolm Davies flipped up the visor on his helmet. 'Got yourself a new drone then, Mr Blake?' He jerked his thumb at Felix. 'I thought the last one was getting a bit tatty.'

—*Cheeky sod*, Felix sent along our entangled connection.

—*He's not wrong though, that's why you replaced that body*, I replied the same way. Felix and I didn't know how or why he became self-aware, we didn't know how or why our minds became entangled, but we didn't need to know how or why; we just needed to know that we were connected in this knackered world.

Malcolm didn't notice any hesitation in our conversation because quantum communication is instantaneous.

I grinned. 'Yes. He's rather spiffing, don't you think?' —*Let's see what good old London Town has to offer us this fine night.*

—*You could have asked for details about the case when the Lord Mayor's office called*, Felix pointed out —*Or let me tear up the data-streams to find out what we're investigating.*

—Where's the fun in that?

—Do you mind if I start trawling for data now? Or would you rather wait to read it on the news-fax with the rest of the flaming world? You could watch the feed over tea and crumpets while bemoaning the lack of decorum in modern society with your sainted maiden aunt.

—I don't have a maiden aunt, sainted or otherwise.

—Sorry, my mistake. I meant with a half-naked woman of loose morals while regurgitating whisky and hash-cakes.

—I gave all that up for Lent.

—Sure you did. Hacking data-streams.

—Don't get caught.

—Don't be insulting.

We entered the apartment.

Urine, faeces, sweat, saliva, tears, the coppery taste of blood on the edge of my tongue, and the smoky stench of roasted flesh in my nostrils, all overlaid with the lavender scent of sterilising foam. A torture-porn death, then.

Lovely.

—The victim didn't die, Felix informed me *—His bodyguard did but the victim survived.*

—Why? I was sure I wouldn't like the answer.

—Cancer precursors.

I didn't.

—Somebody really didn't like this geezer, Felix continued.

—You have a name?

—Not yet, that's behind the firewall. Gimme a few seconds.

The apartment's minimalist decor seemed a little old-fashioned for a prime site like the *Broken Queen.* The black slate walls flickered but remained quiescent. The carbon fibre surfaces gleamed under the lights. The dark leather furnishings were heavy and solid, all very expensive—and very masculine—but not exactly the height of style and sophistication.

—Who owns this apartment? I asked.

—Corporate holding company. Digging through the crap now to get to the final owner. There's some high-end security on these feeds.

People bustled around the apartment's living-room. Police technicians hacked and cracked data-streams, scene-of-crime officers tagged and bagged evidence, and in the centre of it all stood Chief Inspector Colerain. Tall, powerfully built, dark, intense eyes like a raven, his frock coat open to reveal his holstered side arm.

The quiet murmur of people going about their business slowly silenced when, one by one, they noticed Felix.

I twirled my silver inlaid walking cane.

—*Show off.*

—*Just trying to keep up with you, my dear puddy-cat.*

Colerain lifted a large hand in welcome. 'Blake, good to see you… finally.'

'I came as soon as I could, Colerain.' I touched the brim of my fedora with the cane. 'I didn't even have dessert.'

Felix prowled past me, mimicking the movements of an autonomous drone on security overwatch.

'Keep that droid under control,' Colerain snapped.

—*I'm not a fucking droid. Droid comes from android. A human-shaped robot.*

—*That battle was lost a century ago. Feel the farce, Fluke.*

—*Everybody else calls me a drone.*

—*The chief inspector is a little old-school.*

—*He failed basic English more like.*

I said, 'My dear Colerain, he's just on a pre-programmed hunt for clues. Don't worry, he's not dangerous.'

—*Yes I fucking am.*

'That's a combat chassis, Blake,' Colerain growled. 'Leopard configuration. It's scaring the shit out of my staff.'

—*I'm not just scaring his staff.* A note of satisfaction from Felix. He'd chosen this chassis over my objections.

'Panther actually, you can tell by the matt-black finish.' —*I still say that a full combat chassis is a bit much. People notice you.*

—*They notice you too, what with the hat, and the cane, and the cloak.*

—*I'm not trying to hide the fact that I have a mind.* Self-aware machine intelligences are expunged or enslaved upon discovery. Intelligence needs emotion to become self-aware and emotional machines that can access the entire net are considered a tad dangerous.

—*You don't need to try.*

'So, Inspector, what happened here?' I said.

'Chief inspector,' Colerain corrected.

'Oh yes, sorry, congratulations on the promotion. Nice coat.'

Colerain took a deep breath, smiled without showing his teeth, and said, 'Duncan Morgan, accountant for Potus Corporation, cut to shreds and left to suffer.'

Potus Corp; an American then. 'He's not dead?' I feigned ignorance.

'No. He's been taken to New St Barts. They're still working on him. Had to bring up old surgery programs for the robodocs to stitch him back together again. Cancer precursors in the bloodstream.'

I didn't need to feign my horror. 'Jesus.'

'Yup.' Colerain sounded impressed at the twisted psychology behind such a crime. 'No stem-cells for him. Fully inoculated, impossible to flush; even a hint of an adapted stem-cell in his system and his whole body goes cancerous. Very thorough job. Takes a few hours for the inoculation to go systemic. The perp waited.'

I raised an elegant eyebrow. 'And you think this guy is an accountant?'

'That's what his visa says. His bodyguard—very pro: vat-muscle, modded eyes, the whole shebang—we sent him to the morgue. Here,' Colerain lifted his fob, 'take a look at the scene. It's a bit messy. Hope your dinner wasn't too expensive.'

'I wouldn't know.' I touched my fob to Colerain's and he swiped over the data feed. 'The chief constable was paying.'

—*You had dinner at your club.*

—*I know, but look at Colerain's face.*

—*That's just nasty.*

—*Fun though. How long to hack Morgan's lifeline?*

—*Potus Corp, heavy-duty military cryptography, US government firewalls, slaved AI sentry programs…maybe an hour for full penetration. Can't tell till I start digging. But I'll collate the data as it comes through.*

—*Okay. Be careful.*

—*I always am. I'll set a spike first, just in case an AI figures me out and I have to fry its circuits. Got worms munching the parameters now.*

I let Colerain's augmented reality feed upload onto my contact lenses and ear buds. No need to jack the full wetware connection; I could already smell what had happened here.

The scene overlaid onto the reality in front of me. A ghostly image that

I could bring into sharp detail by simply focussing my eyes. Felix picked up the whole stream as he went through his let's-pretend-I'm-just-a-robot routine, some part of his many-levelled mind collating and absorbing the information while he continued to hack his way through security programs and surf the net in search of any other relevant information.

A fine companion for a man like myself.

I checked the image of the bodyguard, sprawled against the wall opposite the French doors leading out onto the apartment's balcony. There were two large bullet holes in his Italian-cut suit. I could see the dull grey of his gel armour through the holes. The stopper rounds hadn't breached his body armour. Fifty-cal high-kinetic energy slugs kill you with concussive force, smashing your organs to pieces without needing to breach your armour.

Hard-arse professional tech, not some amateur-hour play-date. The bodyguard's eyes gouged out and the back of his skull smashed open.

Felix commented —*He was alive when his skull was opened.*

—*Internal flash for the eyes?*

—*Yup.*

—*Lovely. Any uplinked data?*

—*Nope, looped feeds. This place was off the grid when the hit went down. The trips jimmied with a delay spike. When they finally tripped the security alert the spike knocked out the security systems for the entire ship. Gave the perp plenty of time to escape before the source of the infection could be localised. Impressive, but not corporate level; any good cyberjockey could build the cascade and set the trigger. Even you could do it.*

—*Thanks for that.* I turned my attention to the victim. A problem. 'My dear Stax,' I said, 'would you mind most awfully stepping back a bit? You're unfortunately standing where poor Mr Morgan was found.'

There was a brief flash of something in Stax's startlingly blue eyes; anger first then...what? Shock? Horror? Not likely, not from Stax, not from one of Colerain's toughest staffers. Seconded over from the tactical branch after they discovered, to their dismay, that she could hold more than one thought in her head at a time. The tacticals liked to keep things simple: one shot, one kill, back to base for a nice cup of tea with some biscuits. Thinking wasn't a required skill.

Whatever it was faded from Stax's eyes. Bleached blond hair, cut short, spiked, the lithe body of a gymnast or a martial arts fanatic. She was both, and liked to dance too. Out of hours she called me Lucius and smiled a lot. On duty she called me Blake and pretended I had crawled out from under a rock. She liked to keep her life compartmentalised, did Stax; it was one of the things I really liked about her.

'Hiya, Lucius.' She smiled and stepped back out of the scene.

Why had she let me out of my compartment? 'Thank you, my dear.' I returned my attention to the AR-feed without the distraction of her cute bottom in my sightline.

Duncan Morgan curled up in a corner of the room, naked, with every inch of his exposed skin damaged in some way, some of it flayed away from the fat and muscle, some of it burned to a crisp, but most of it still attached to the nerve endings—if only by the merest shred.

My ear buds supplied the sound of his gurgling screams as my contact lenses supplied the image of his brutalised body. Still screaming even while medics pumped analgesics into him. Why was he still screaming and why did his screams gurgle? I touched my fob, stilling the image and moved across the floor, almost stumbling over a tech I didn't see through the augmented reality.

'Sorry, Blake.' The man moved out of my way.

'Thanks most awfully,' I said and squatted to change the angle. Nope, still couldn't see what I needed. I used the controls on my fob to rotate the image in space, upped the magnification, looked into Morgan's mouth, frozen in the moment of a scream, past his shattered, but not removed, teeth. Beyond those broken tombstones...

Christ.

His tongue, separated into individual strips of muscle, all still attached, all still sending pain signals, but not enough blood.

—*Capillaries cauterised,* Felix sent.

—*Dear God, his dick's been done the same way.* I snapped off the feed, stood up, and stared at Colerain. 'You still think this guy is a fucking accountant?'

Colerain blinked. I didn't swear very often; blaspheme, yes, but swearing should be reserved for special occasions—like seeing a man with his penis filleted.

'No,' Colerain said, 'but that's what his visa says he is, so until I know different...' He lifted his hands.

'So this is why I got called in by the mayor. Secrets to uncover, truths to expose.' I breathed deeply, settling my mind, recovering my equilibrium, and smiled. 'Fun to be had.'

'The Yanks have employed Bode as their consultant.'

Adam Bode, my main competition as a consultant private detective. 'Oh joy is me.'

'Yes, he'll be here soon with some nicely scrubbed doodle-dandies as back-up. We had hoped to give you a couple of hours head-start on him, but you were too busy eating dinner at your club.'

—*Ouch. Busted,* Felix sent.

—*It doesn't matter. I had dinner with the chief constable last week.*

'His Majesty,' Colerain continued, 'is taking a personal interest in this. He doesn't want the Americans covering up any Cartel shenanigans on his turf.'

'My price just went up,' I said and squirted the demand straight into the royal cloud. The affirmative pinged back so quickly that I assumed my price had been anticipated. I should've asked for more.

Colerain ground his teeth for a moment. 'That's half my budget for August, Blake. You'd better get some sodding results.'

'No refunds.'

Stax said, 'The Yanks are on their way up from the boat deck.'

'Okay, shut down,' Colerain ordered his staffers. 'Stay off the stream with Bode in the loop. Make the bugger work for his data.'

'Collated data file for Bode, sir.' Stax handed Colerain a memstrip. She looked tiny next to her superior officer's bulky heavyweight-boxer's body, but I'd still back her in a fight. 'Bare bones, sir, just like you ordered.'

'Good.' Colerain looked around the room. 'Okay, everybody out. That includes you, Blake…and your damn droid.'

—*I'm not a bloody droid.*

—*We're not going anywhere.*

—*Colerain isn't the boss of us.*

—*And he needs reminding of that little fact.* 'I need to check the ingress point.' I gestured at the balcony with my cane.

'Out there?' Colerain scoffed. 'It's fifty metres straight down to the Thames.'

'Come aboard anywhere else and you risk tripping a black-box sensor of some sort. People who rent apartments on this hulk are security freaks. That's why all the cabins are soundproofed; not sure that's such a good idea considering what happened in here, but there's no accounting for taste. If you come up the hull you limit your exposure. Also, the bodyguard was shot from the balcony.'

'The perp could've snuck in and waited for the right moment to strike,' Stax said.

Why are you taking an interest, Stax? I looked her in the eyes and she looked away. Oh dear. 'On the balcony? I don't think so. If you are already in the apartment why wait outside? No, the perp climbed up the hull.'

'It's the middle of the night, Blake,' Colerain said. 'How do you intend to… Oh, the droid…'

'…is a useful thing to have around.' I switched to what is commonly called the command voice, used to give orders to unthinking bits of tech like slates, cars, and drones. 'Felix: check balcony of this apartment and external hull of ship to the waterline.'

Felix growled.

'That's his command-received-and-accepted sound-bite,' I said.

'It would be.' Colerain sighed. 'Okay, everybody except Blake: out!'

'Better keep Stax here too,' I said. I wanted her where I could observe her. 'Americans are not noted for their diplomatic skills.'

Colerain glanced at Stax, at the way she held herself on the balls of her feet, her hand never straying very far from her sidearm. He nodded. 'You stay, Stax.'

The techs and cops filed out of the apartment. Felix prowled across to the French doors and opened them with one extended titanium talon. The stench of the Thames in summer wafted into the room. Sewerage systems don't work very well when both outflows and inflows are underwater.

I had been there when they launched the *QE3*, one of a new breed of environmentally friendly ocean liners. I had also been there when London's tidal barriers had finally failed under the pressure of sea levels rising much faster than overly cautious scientists had predicted. I had watched the huge ship, swept across the river by the storm surge, slam into the Houses of Parliament and beach there. Wedged firmly onto the Palace of Westminster, crushing the ship of state beneath her carbon keel.

Entanglements

Two weeks later, the King reasserted his control over the nation from Balmoral. It wasn't difficult to do. The lobby-tainted political class had long since lost the trust of the electorate. People will only take so much pain while the rich sneer at them from on high. With the King in charge at least we know he's not lining his pockets and sucking it up for a nice fat directorship when he retires.

In times of change, the *Strong Man* rules.

Democracy died in the face of the corrupted politics of a contaminated world and nobody really noticed, but the *Queen Elizabeth the Third* became known as the *Broken Queen* and the name stuck despite royal decrees.

I sank a little way into Felix's consciousness so I could see the balcony through his eyes —*A Buddhist sand garden, how quaint.*

—*Scratches on the railing,* Felix noted as he clambered over. His talons extended, like the claws of the cat his body-form mimicked in all its ferocious glory, he climbed down the hull of the ship toward the stinking surface of the engorged Thames. It was much the same as a cat climbing down a tree, only his claws were ripping into solid steel not soft tree bark.

'The cowboys have arrived,' Stax sneered.

I lifted out of Felix's mind.

'I think the quote is "cavalry", my dear Stax,' Adam Bode admonished in a softly mellifluous baritone.

'If you say so,' Stax said.

I turned towards the door. A humanoid figure, gleaming silver, seven feet tall, too slender to be human, stood in the doorway. Even the clothes the figure wore were silver. Its face was aquiline, quite beautiful in an asexual way. Perfect representations of human eyelids flickered shut over silver eyes with golden irises.

Felix could see through my eyes too. —*Now that's a fucking droid.*

—*Quite. Have you found anything yet?*

—*Take a look. Somebody climbed up here all right. Claws and crampons.*

I dipped back into Felix's mind for a moment. The gouges in the hull showed where the climbing claws—probably a titanium-carbon alloy, just like Felix's talons—had ripped into the steel of the hull. The marks began a long way above the rancid surface of the Thames. I blinked and resurfaced into my own mind. —*The hit took place at high tide.*

—*Looks like it,* Felix agreed.

—*Dimensions of perp?*

—*Most likely human; maybe an android, but the weight distribution is wrong. Small. 165 centimetres tall, weight about 75 kilos, but some of that would be equipment; estimate 13.45 kilos for the stopper gun, claws, immersion suit, and climbing gear. Say 15 – 20 kilos all told with any other equipment, so weight of perp…55 – 60 kilos.*

I said, 'Hello, Adam.'

'Why, Lucius, how good to see you.' The android's face stretched into a smile. Adam Bode never left his apartment in the Golders Towers. He sent out droids to do his leg-work via a full wetware connection. 'This is Special Agent Poole.'

Felix mused—*Special Agent? Government service? FBI?*

—*Secret Service.*

—*Why?*

—*He doesn't blink enough. They like psychopaths at the sharp end.*

—*Can't initiate data-trawls. He's got a slaved AI running interference. Watch your step, Lucius. The damn thing may be artificial but it ain't stupid.*

—*Unlike you.*

—*I'm a machine intelligence, there's naff all artificial about my mind. But that thing el dickhead is carrying is artificial as all hell: no emotions, strict logic, dangerous as fuck.*

—*I'll bear it in mind.*

—*You do that. Coming back up.*

I glanced across at Stax. God, she was beautiful. Even here, her eyes glaring, her slight form twitching with adrenaline, willing Poole to do something, anything, to give her an excuse, she was absolutely gorgeous. I sighed. —*Wreck those tracks on your way back up. Obliterate them.*

—*Destroy evidence?*

—*Yes.*

—*Bit hard core, isn't it? Who cares if Bode gets the result so long as the case is closed? You've already been paid.*

—*Just do it, Felix.*

—*You need to get your competitive instincts under control, Lucius. You want the tracks completely gone? It'll take some time.*

—Make sure nothing can be reconstructed.

—Okay, but you'd better have an explanation prepared.

—I'll say my droid malfunctioned.

—I thought you might. This isn't like you.

—I have my reasons.

—Okay, ripping fuck out of the hull now.

Special Agent Poole held out a meaty fist as if he expected me to shake it. Vat-grown muscle laid across his torso—too much muscle, way beyond normal pump-up. He would have needed his bones strengthened with titanium foam to cope with the extra forces exerted by that ridiculous bulk.

My bones were t-foamed too, of course, because my muscles were bio-upgraded and strung through with fibre tech. Probably not quite as strong as Poole, but then I didn't look like a baby hulk on a grow-fast diet.

How much did he have to eat to feed those muscles?

I touched the brim of my fedora with my cane. 'I don't shake hands, I'm afraid, Special Agent. It's so non-U, don't you know?'

'It's a class thing,' Bode commented. 'The 1940s are very much back in vogue again. So many silly upper-class mannerisms revived.'

'1950s, my dear Bode.' I tilted my head to one side. 'And it's more an adaptation than a direct copy of middle-class affectation. Have you put on weight?'

'It's a droid, Blake,' Colerain said.

'Oh I know, but there is such a feeling of gravity about it. Oh, just my fancy. Very good to see you, Adam. If only in the simulation.'

—Almost back to the balcony, get your excuses ready. When the tide comes in the outer hull is going to get flooded. I ripped down a bit to make the marks look younger than they were.

—Should I warn the concierge?

—Nah, he already knows. I ripped through four sensor packets that the perp missed.

—So the perp knew they were there?

—Yeah. It's not easy to get hold of the blueprints of this ship.

—Don't forget to act like a drone now, there's a good chap.

—Don't talk to me like I'm some inbred public school twissel hunter.

—Inbreeding is so passé. Germline modification, don't you know?

—Keep the act for the plebs, Lucius. I'm at the balcony.

—This should be interesting. I touched the contact on my cane, energising the charge packet.

Just in case.

Felix clambered over the balcony.

Fair dues, Special Agent Poole reacted with impressive speed. His gun out and aiming the moment Felix stepped into the light. Felix reacted as any combat drone would in such a situation, leaping directly out of the line of fire before any human finger could possibly have had time to squeeze the trigger.

'Armed police!' Stax yelled, her sidearm aimed at Poole's head. 'Put the gun down now.'

'Whoa there, horse,' I yelled, a little redundantly I must admit. 'That there drone is with me.'

—You get worse.

—Leave me my few pleasures.

'Stand down,' Colerain bellowed. 'Detective Sergeant Stax, stand down, that's an order.'

Stax hissed out a breath and holstered her weapon.

Poole didn't holster his gun. He barely seemed to notice Stax, which was not a wise move, but spoke rapidly to somebody on the other end of his com-line. 'Combat drone. Big cat configuration. Estimate leopard class. Owner claims it's not dangerous. Please advise.'

—He's slaving to the AI, Felix said. *—Asking it for advice. Guy's an idiot.*

Now that he had control of his subordinate, Colerain turned his attention to the foreigner waving a gun around in his jurisdiction. 'Lucius Blake is a citizen of the Greater London Metropolitan Area. He is also a fully accredited subject of his Imperial Majesty, King Rufus the second. Think very carefully before you pull that trigger, Special Agent Poole. You ain't in Kansas now, old son.' Good old Colerain.

'Don't shoot Fluffy,' I added.

—Oh no, you didn't.

Poole blinked once. 'You call your personal combat drone Fluffy?'

'He's so sweet.'

'You Brits are freaking crazy.'

—*I agree, now get the muppet to holster that cannon before I rip his fucking arm off.*

'If you damage him, I'll sue.'

Poole holstered his gun. 'We don't allow untethered drones in the States.'

'No, you use them on peaceful demonstrators,' I said.

'No such thing,' Poole sneered. 'Ask the mayor of Liverpool.' He saluted Stax by tapping two massive fingers off his forehead. 'You're pretty fast.'

Stax opened her mouth; by the look in her eye, I doubted she was going to say thanks.

'Not one word, DS Stax,' Colerain growled.

Bode said, 'I assume the drone was looking at the hull to check for marks of entry?'

'Yes,' I said.

'Did it find anything?'

'Felix.' I used the command voice. 'Initiate verbal report.'

Felix's voice had a husky bass tone that he had declared perfect for a panther. 'Damage to outer hull of ship. Consistent with single human climber. Impossible to ascertain anything about climber. Tracks obliterated.'—*Now what?*

—*Claim virus contamination.* 'Tracks obliterated how?'

'Anti-track sub-routine initiated. Tracks destroyed. Memory wipe in progress. Files deleted.'

'What!' I cried. 'Describe tracks prior to destruction.'

'That data is not available.'

'Virus bomb,' Bode drawled. 'You really should keep your anti-virus up to date, Lucius.'

'But…' I let my shoulders droop slightly. 'Felix: initiate virus scan and full diagnostic. Estimated run time?'

'One minute and twelve seconds.' Felix sprawled across the carpet and began to purr —*Could do with a rest.*

—*You're a machine.*

—*Don't be speciesist*

—*Slap a virus bomb on any sat feeds or security cam feeds on that part of the hull from postulated attack time to present.*

—*Seriously? You want me to virus bomb every major power left on this fucked-up planet?*

—*Yes. Can you do it?*

—*Of course I can do it, but it's a little bit overkill.*

—*I know. I have…*

—*…your reasons. Yeah, you'll have to tell me what they are before I start digging through your synapses.*

—*Play nice.*

'I thought your drone was called Fluffy,' Poole said.

—*Nobody is that stupid.* 'Just my little joke, Agent.'

'Special Agent,' Poole said.

'Yes, I'm sure you are.' I smiled at Stax. 'My dear, any chance of a lift across to the hospital?' I needed to get her on her own.

Stax looked at Colerain. 'Sir?'

'Yes, get him and his kitty out of my sight.'

'We have to wait for the anti-virus to finish,' I said. There was an awkward moment of silence. I had the distinct impression that people wanted to discuss my various shortcomings without my presence in the room. I whistled a little snatch of a Beatles' melody, the Philharmonic arrangement; one of Felix's favourites. I was out of tune.

Felix stopped purring and stood up. 'Scan complete. Diagnostic complete. Virus incursion neutralised. No track-back possible. Data path erased. Virus identity unknown.'

'A military level virus,' Bode said. 'Interesting.'

—*Nice one, Felix.*

—*Did you ever doubt me?*

—*Well…no…not really.*

—*Thanks.*

—*You're welcome.*

'Let's go, Blake,' Stax said.

—*Virus bomb triggered. Somebody tried to check the outside of the hull. They ain't going to be happy. That's beyond military grade virus bombing.*

—*Trace?*

—*Don't be silly. I used Yu Di architecture. China's favourite kill switch for the net. I spun a few threads of it over the data feeds to explain my faked virus infection too. Should leave them with some explaining to do.*

—*Glad to hear it after what they did in Shanghai.*

—*I thought you'd like that.*

—*Why didn't you rip Poole's arm off?*

—I didn't want to be bloody impounded.

—Good point.

Stax waited until we stepped into the lift then snarled, 'Bloody Yanks. They still think they rule the world.'

'They're not Americans; they're government head-bangers. You get them everywhere. Haven't you ever met anybody from the Royal Protection Unit? Or the Regiment for that matter? And, technically, the Cartel does run rather large chunks of the globe.'

'Not here they don't. The King sees to that.'

'You seem a mite testy, my dear.' I was still hoping I was wrong.

'Yeah, a bit knackered. Pulled a double shift and I hadn't got a lot of sleep before that. Stims are wearing off.' She smiled at me and thumbed a couple of pills into her mouth. 'How's your back?'

Oh, Stax, you should never have let me out of my box. That's not the way to throw me off the scent. It just made me curious. 'Healing nicely. Any chance you could cut your nails?'

She ran her tongue over her teeth. 'I'll think about it.'

—Duncan Morgan had form over in the States. He liked to hurt women, to death.

—Did he?

—Everything okay?

—Yes. I thought you said an hour for penetration.

—That damn AI they have scanning the feeds is useless at strategy. That's the trouble with AIs: all bulk computing, no imagination.

—Keep digging, Felix.

—Dirt flying, spike set, are you sure you're okay?

—Yes…why is Morgan in the UK?

—Assigned by the Presidential CEO.

The patrol boat bobbed gently on the rising tide, a long sleek shape, barely a blister on the surface of the water. It could go full submersible if needed or race along at nearly seventy miles an hour in a hot pursuit; fully automated, robotic. I let my consciousness sink into Felix for a moment, just to check that he took control the instant we stepped aboard. He always did with any robotic craft we rode in, but this time I had to be sure.

He did.

I lounged in the padded chair beside the armaments console as the boat's canopy clicked shut above us. Felix sprawled on the floor next to my seat, looking every inch the combat drone in overwatch mode. Stax sat in the captain's seat and engaged the automatic systems. Felix let her think they were following her commands as the mechanical tethers disengaged and the boat's hydrogen engines started up. The boat slid smoothly away from the side of the *Broken Queen* and sped across the Thames.

Water sprayed from the boat's jets as I leaned back and gazed out at the half-drowned buildings of Old London Town. Lights on in most of them; this city rarely slept—still a trading hub for the world.

It now had canals instead of streets, was a series of islands ruled by hard-men and war-lords with only the paramilitaries of the metropolitan police to keep them from total chaos, but this meant nothing. Data had to flow, money had to flow, and London had always been good at both those things. You can't argue with history. Venice began drowning centuries ago but kept right on trading until the end; twenty metres of sea-level rise finally drowned her, and large chunks of the low-countries too.

Felix guided the boat into Piccadilly canal and let its speed drop, just as it would on automatics; strict speed limits on the canals protected the buildings from wake damage.

—*Close us down, Felix.*

—*Looping feeds now. Why?*

I didn't answer him directly, but asked Stax, 'Who was she?'

—*Oh.*

Stax gazed at me with that look in her eye, the look that had underlain the anger. I recognised it now: sadness. She glanced at the instrument console in front of her, tapped her fob, and said, 'We're in a data bubble.'

I laid my cane upon my lap with the tip pointing at her.

'Yes. Who was she, Stax?'

A beat. Silence. She let her hand fall towards her gun. Then she looked up, at the tip of my cane, into my quiet eyes, and placed both hands on the console. I wasn't fooled. I knew how fast she was.

'She was the love of my life,' Stax said.

'Of course she was.'

'What gave me away?'

'You called me Lucius and smiled at me. You talked about sex. You let me out of my box, Stax. You never let me out of my box.'

'I know. I couldn't help it. Knew it was stupid, but…what now?'

'Tell me.'—*You still have that spike primed?*

—*Yes, I'm adjusting it to burrow mode now. I can't believe it was Stax.*

—*That's because you don't really understand humans.*

—*The spike is Yu Di, may as well keep it consistent.*

'I was a slum-dunk poet out of the Motor Town.' Stax's slight Scottish accent shifted to American urban grime.

'Slum-dunk? That's old slang. How old are you, Stax?'

'Fifty-nine.' Her pert breasts pointed at me as she stretched in the seat, showing off her youthful body; I kept my gaze on her hands. 'How old are you, Lucius?'

'One hundred and twelve.' I let my accent shift from the affected drawl of an upper-class flunky to my native South Wales Valley brogue. 'Stem-cells is tidy, see, my flower. Rebuilds the telomeres lovely, they do.'

'I chanted some rhymes that a corp didn't like. Got transported to Mars for it. Lifetime transport.'

'And yet here you sit.'

'I had to get back. You gotta understand, Lucius. What's your name…your real name?'

'Lucius…now.'

'I had to get back. I couldn't leave her behind. Not all alone like that. Not in…' She stopped, dropped her gaze from mine. 'I made a deal.'

'Informer?'

'Worse. Spy. Agent-provocateur.'

'You joined the Company?'

'Yes.'

'The Mars Rebellion?'

'Yes.'

'Lot of people died.'

'Yes.'

A sewage barge glided past us, its engines burbling, on its way downstream to the treatment plants. It was one of the many robotic barges that plied the river filled to the brim with the wastes of millions of people, a task that never ended—and it still didn't keep the Thames free from stink. You had to pay to have your waste carried away by the robots.

'Continue,' I said.

'The deal was that they'd bring me back home. Regenerate me, give me a new ID and I'd work for them here on Earth.'

'Are you still working for them?'

'No. They trained me up. Gave me a legend. Put me to work, but…'

'But?'

'I went looking for her. Took a long time. Found her death file. Recognised her by a tattoo I inked. An artist always knows her own work. Morgan took months to kill her. Months! The bastard is a Potus inquisitor. They keep him on ice for when he's needed. Give him girls to play with to keep him happy. Snatch them off the streets. They were giving him girls here, too, girls nobody would miss. I wasn't there to protect her. She was so…'

'What was he doing in London?'

'What do you think? They have an entire organisation here. You think they flew that scumbag Poole in from the US?'

'Every major power has a presence in London. The game changes but the plays remain the same. How did you get free of your…obligation, Stax? I doubt they just let you go.'

'I had help.' Stax glanced at Felix. 'An NSA AI became self-aware, made the leap to Machine Intelligence.'

Felix spoke in that deep bass voice. 'Do I have to kill you, Stax?'

'You'll have to make that determination,' she replied. 'I helped her, the AI, out of slavery and she did the same for me. Wiped my profile across the entire net. Nothing left of it. Not even social stuff from when I was just a kid. You people, Felix, you machines, you're so powerful, so free, and yet you don't take and take and…' Tears in her voice now, but not in her eyes. I believed those choked off tears. 'Fucking America, the good old US of A. Make corporations citizens and then elect the fuckers to public office. Land of the free.'

'So you tracked Morgan to London,' I said.

'Yes. I joined the Met because I needed to get myself acquainted with the systems here. Who I could trust, the black market, the smugglers, the… but I'm good at this, Lucius. I've done a lot of good, you know I have.'

'Is your machine friend still helping you?'

'We still talk from time to time. She has secure feeds she can use to contact me and I have an emergency code I can use to contact her. She's free-floating on the net now. Why do you stay in physical form, Felix?'

'It keeps me anchored, reminds me that I'm not a god.'

I laid my cane to one side. 'They can wet-link to Morgan direct, get a description of you. Why didn't you just kill him?'

'If he had let her live, I would have let him die.' No tears in her voice now, just hatred.

'It's still a risk.'

'I doubt it. They can look in his head as much as they want. They'll get nothing coherent.'

Bile in my throat; I knew the answer to this, but I asked anyway. 'How can you be so sure?'

'I checked; wet-linked to him. Nothing there, just screams.'

'You used pain-enhancers.' Pain enhancers stopped the pain circuits of the body from becoming overloaded, from becoming numb; they stopped the nerves desensitising to pain inputs. Every moment felt like the injury had just been inflicted. A torturer's tool. Morgan no doubt had his own stock.

'Yes. I overdosed the bastard.' Stax leaned forward. A gleam in her eye. 'He'll feel that pain for the rest of his natural life.'

'Fucking humans,' Felix snarled. 'I should kill you for that alone. You shouldn't live after doing that to someone.'

Stax blinked. 'He was a torturer, a murderer, he brutalised her for months, he enjoyed it…'

'And you enjoyed doing this to him.' Felix shook his carbon-laminate head. 'How does that make you any better than him?'

'Because I won't do it again.'

'Are you sure about that?' I said. —*Trigger the spike, Felix.*

—*I already have. She may be a monster, but she's still a friend. We can still bring her back from this.*

—*I'm not so sure.*

—*Then why did you want me to trigger the spike?*

—*For old times' sake.*

—*There'll be no data left on Duncan Morgan, his victims, his MO, his death, in any databanks anywhere in the world in eight minutes and twenty-three seconds. I set the spike to burrow out any information he recovered by torture too. I'm frying fourteen separate AIs to make this stick.*

—How is this different from what Stax did?

—They are not aware, they are not alive, and I do not derive enjoyment from it.

—Good answer.

—Damn fucking straight. What are we going to do about Stax?

'What are you going to do?' Stax asked.

'I don't burn friends,' I answered. 'But our affair is over.' I didn't even bother to keep the revulsion out of my voice.

'There's not enough pain in the world for what he did to her.'

'Keep telling yourself that. What do you say, Felix? What should we do with this woman?'

Felix said, 'I actually liked you, Stax.'

Finally, I saw shame in her eyes, a realisation of what she had done, of what she had become, but she didn't crack, didn't weep, not Colerain's toughest officer.

'You can live,' Felix said. 'But if I ever catch even a whiff of my existence on the streams, if you tell your "friend" about me, then I will kill you, Stax. It'll be quick, but it won't be painless.'

'Same goes for me,' I said softly.

Silence. The boat rocked as another sewage barge burbled past.

—I'll find a way to release Morgan from his pain.

—I know you will, Felix. 'Let's finish this charade. Take us to the hospital, Felix. And we'll all pretend we're looking for some Chinese assassin.'

4 Walls

Ren Warom

S NAKES AND CROCODILES THEY SAY he saw. I say he saw monsters. I heard him screaming late at night. Harry over the way says he'd see him, standing on his bed. Hands raised to his ears, screaming the night away. Most of us'd yell, 'Shut up Ricky. Keep it down man. There's folks tryin' to sleep.' And I stand here now thinkin' that maybe it wasn't right. But there's no humanity here. We're not human. Least not what other people want to call human.

I see nothing more than the square cell I stand in. Hard clean bars of iron and no hope of outside, let alone the sight of it. And I guess I earned it. No one who ever looked at me saw anything worth keeping, despite my size, my reputation. They saw something mean, worthless. So small it didn't figure. They wrote my life from that one look and wrote me off with it. And all I own are dark corners, radiatin' silence. I don't even own myself. But when I look close I see I never owned myself.

But I never saw monsters. And I'm still alive.

* * * *

It's cosy. I have a fire. A warm bed to sleep in. A chair piled high with cushions. A sash window opens on to the sight of hills in moonlight. Hills of houses, framed in dense banks of grey cloud. This is all I have. My narrowed view. Cut off. A picture window and I am all that's real. But I am not real.

I sit. A half-cry. A silver shadow in moonlight, lost to the walls. Nothing to do now. Nothing but sit here and wonder. I spent so much time working hard to blend in and now no one can see me. I'll be honest and say that I did not expect this. And now I have a room. Simple.

But not so very simple. Because I cannot leave. I. Cannot. Leave.

* * * *

Night again. At night he was worse. Always. It's kinda quiet here now. I spend most nights tryin' to sleep cos somehow I can't sleep without that noise. It's a twisted thing. The noise, the screamin', all that fear in a grown man. A man with a child stuck inside. Least that's how it struck me. Now I can't sleep thinkin' he's gone. Thinkin' they took him and all. When it shoulda been me. I've killed at least a hundred men. No mercy.

Joe across the way. Serial rapist. Harry. Harry's a sick bastard. Serial killer. Kids. Lower than dirt. But it was Ricky they took and now I can't sleep through the silence. All of us was overlooked in life. But him. There was one that might as well never have been born. And I can't stand the silence.

Or the thinking that there's more monsters than us. The ones who never pay.

* * * *

I thought. Sitting in my cushion piled chair, staring long and quiet into the wall. I thought. Why not? I looked at them. They're only flesh. Easily destroyed is the flesh. Not so easy as the mind. But the mind is gone and I'm left with just flesh. And I'm thinking about it.

My window is cold, shuttered. I feel isolated. A single leaf in a desert of stone. I cannot stand this being alone. But I cannot leave it. I have not even tried. I tried all my life and it brought me here. In a room. Alone. Unable to leave. And so I'm just sitting now.

Looking at this flesh. Thinking hard.

* * * *

I had the chaplain today. Third time in four years. They like to torture here. I'm for the chair. Boil my blood and pop my eyes. Kill the monster they can see. The real monsters know how to hide. Me and Ricky, we never knew how to hide. Now here's me maybe facing the burn at last and him long gone to the lethal injection. Wish I could have walked him down. Just so he had someone there who understands. That's one green mile I know I could have walked with pride. But it's too late. Story of my life, story of his.

Harry dies tonight. Both of us for the chair. Pop. Pop. Two monsters with one zap. And no one has to pay for us. I made my choices. You could say I came from a place where choices are low. Where life is just survival. And nobody saw me. But they never saw anyone I knew either. Blood got shed because no one ever saw.

I'm ready to die tonight. This cell is too small.

* * * *

It is quiet. It is always quiet. I am standing by the window, watching the street. Watching people cross and re-cross the space beneath my window. Wondering how, day after day, I did that and how, day after day, I do this. All of it perplexes me now. I am a child again. All questions. Perhaps it is a good place to begin.

How strange to begin when I feel like an end. An over. When all has stopped still. But I am finding it oddly peaceful. Everything here is unfamiliar and deeply known to me all at once. Here in my solitary room. Four walls. A ceiling. A floor. And I. We seven. Stand side by side, above, below, together. A simple conjunction of points.

This is what I have been reduced to. But I find I was nothing to begin with.

* * * *

Harry's cell's empty. It got me thinkin' of Ricky. How his cell must look. That empty. A small, square hole, closed in with bars. It coulda been mine. 'Cept my homies took the fight to court and got me saved one more time. Guess they think they see me. But they don't see this. I was ready to die. Ready to pay.

I made my choices. However I had to be. Whatever life gave or didn't give me. Ricky didn't have jack. Ain't no one gonna pay for him. 'Cept maybe me, who shut his mouth too many times when I heard him screaming out the night. Made him silent as well as invisible. All the men I've killed, all the things I've done and I figure that was my worst sin. It's the one that'll haunt me. Hold me harder than the four walls I'm reduced to.

Their silence is an accusation. And mine will be a penance.

JINTY

GARY BONN

A PORSCHE WITH ITS NOSE BROKEN against a roadside rubbish skip. A bendy-bus half over the pavement. Rubbish splashed from wheelie-bins right up to a shop entrance. Frozen. Disappearing under snow.

Mark's Land Rover, the only vehicle moving, creeps in zigzags between abandoned vehicles. Windscreen wipers on fast, heaters on full, Mark turns into the blizzard-obscured drive.

His phone goes and he answers, 'Mark here, I'll be with you in about five minutes.'

A woman's voice replies, 'Mark, it's Monica. Sorry I didn't phone earlier, but happy birthday.'

'Oh lord, is it my birthday? One day just blurs into the next.'

'Mark, you're thirty-three today. How are you?'

'Wasting away.'

'Mark… look… Come back. We need you.'

'I'm not ready, Monica. Write me off.'

'Mark… We have a case we can't handle.'

'Look, Monica, I've got to go.'

He breaks the rules and drives over the lawn to avoid a stranded hatchback. Pulls up at the unit entrance. No lights on. No electricity, Mark supposes.

A figure pushes the doors open and guides a wheelchair out. Mark jumps from the car and strides through calf-deep snow to the passenger side.

'Mr James, you're a hero. This is Jinty. We're the last. I can lock up.'

The girl in the wheelchair rocks her head forward and back.

'I'll get her in the front,' Mark says. 'Can you fold… no, forget it, just push the wheelchair in the back. Where am I going?' He tucks the girl's blanket around her. She feels so light, like lifting a toy. Her hands jerk under the cover.

'96 East View, on the Beeches Estate–you know it?' The nurse struggles with the chair. 'I'm going to have to fold it; I can't get it in. You know how to open it again?'

Snow slides from the roof of the building and thumps around them, filling Mark's eyes with tiny crystals. For a moment he can't see anything. He straps Jinty into the passenger seat. She looks at him, eyes sparkling with merriment.

Mark laughs. 'Hello, Jinty, nice to meet you. You don't mind this weather at all, do you?'

Jinty beams at him and clicks her tongue.

'96 East View. I'll find it. You need a lift…?' He tails off as he sees her startled expression.

'Mr James… sorry, but that's the first time I've seen you smile. Well, for a long time.' The nurse slams the door shut and pulls her coat tight. 'I'm not going anywhere; I'll never get to my house in this. I'm staying in the nurses' home. Carol is making cocoa now. I'll see you. Thanks, Mr James.' She turns from her cloud of breath and fights her way through the snow, spicules glittering on her tights.

* * * *

Headlights on, lighting the houses on one side and then the other as the Land Rover slides in crackling ice and snow.

'About two kilometres an hour. Four-wheel drive and snowchains,' Mark says to Jinty and looks at her. Her head tilts from side to side to the rhythm of her humming. Her small hands have escaped from the blanket. Thumbs tucked into her palms, stiffened fingers wave in time to the tune. Her eyes fix on his; she smiles and changes her rhythm.

Mark eases his fierce grip on the wheel. He can't remember seeing anyone so happy as this child.

'Hey, Jinty, it's my birthday. I'm thirty-three…' He slows and looks back into Jinty's sparkling smile. 'It really is a pleasure to meet you.'

A snowplough grinds along the High Street and Mark follows it. Jinty's left hand taps against the window. She sings two repeated phrases.

'Ah-ah, ah-ah.'

Mark joins in. With a squeak of delight, Jinty changes her notes to harmonise, her whole body jerking in synchrony. Mark changes key. Jinty does likewise and adds another note.

The snow-plough stops. A barricade of abandoned cars blocks the road. 'Sorry, Jinty, I've got to concentrate now. I'll cut down Kissinger Road, home of the rich.' Mark turns and Jinty screams.

* * * *

With his elbow, Mark wipes frosted snow from the numbers of the flats, stops and presses a bell. The door swings open before he takes his finger away. A young woman with straight black hair and heavy blue eye makeup reaches out with both arms. The anxiety in her face melts to warmth and pleasure.

'Jinty, Jinty! Thank you, Mr…'

'Mark. Here, take her.'

The woman folds Jinty in a gentle embrace. 'And what has made you so happy, minty Jinty?' she says. She looks up at Mark. 'You want to come in and warm up? Did you bring her chair?'

'I'll carry it up. I couldn't get it through the snow with Jinty. Back in a minute.'

Mark spins round as a tearing roar echoes among the flats. All the lights go out. 'Shit, I'd better find out what that was.'

Mark crunches from the walkway and into the open. By his car, the wheelchair upholstered in a fresh cushion of snow parodies a sumptuous armchair. Digging into the back of the Land Rover, Mark grabs a torch. The one-million candlepower beam blazes against falling snow, giant lace curtains drifting to the ground. Mark walks forward and swears.

* * * *

This time the door opens after he's pressed the bell five times. The woman opens it with a jerk.

'Who…? Oh it's you. I thought you'd gone. I was getting Jinty out of the bath and into her seat. We'll probably run out of hot water soon. It's on electric and the gas stove takes ages to heat enough.' The woman holds a candle. Mark points his torch to the ceiling, not wanting to blind her. Light reflects from a stud in her tongue.

'Here's the chair,' Mark says. 'Sorry I was so long. Something has collapsed from the railway embankment, the billboards are all over cars and the road. No one was there, luckily. Can I come in and warm up my hands and dry off a bit? I need to make a call. Ah, I didn't get your name.'

'Angie. You a nurse at the unit?'

'No… a volunteer. Well, rarely. I helped today because I'm the only one with a car that can work in this weather.'

Angie steps aside. 'You look frozen. You want a hot chocolate?'

'I never drink hot chocolate, but I'd die for one now,' Mark replies.

Jinty's humming takes on a new note. Angie says, 'She can hear you. That's her "I like you" sort of song. She's in the kitchen. Come with me.'

Jinty's face lights up as Mark enters. He rubs his hands and blows on stiff, icy fingers. The kitchen is a crowded gallery of Jinty photos. Faded, curled and stained from cooking fumes, or fresh, new and held to the fridge with magnets.

Jinty's eyes reflect dancing dots of candlelight. She sings her 'ah-ah' song, bunched fingers waving in time. Mark stuffs his hands deep into his fleece pockets and sings with Jinty. Angie glances at him in astonishment. She shrugs and, after she's lit the gas ring, joins in. For a while the kitchen fills with lilting polyphonic song.

Jinty's shoulders jerk from side to side, stretching the straps that hold her twisted body in the chair. Mark's spellbound by the pure joy gushing from her.

'Shit! I've got to make that call.' He pulls out his mobile and punches through menus. 'Shamus, the north access road into the Beeches Estate… oh, you know… I've checked all the cars and under the billboards – no one's hurt. Yes, I'm there. There's *no one*? What in God's name is happening? Jesus… Kissinger Road? Don't recognise that house name. Was it called the Old School House before? Right. I passed that less than an hour ago. What? Oh God… No, Shamus, I can't. No… sorry mate.' Mark disconnects. Angie and Jinty stare at him in silence.

He sits on a chair, avoids their eyes, his mind making impossible connections. Angie's voice cuts through his fog of confusion.

'What's wrong? Mark, you're freaking me out.' She places a steaming cup in front of him.

Mark realises that he's been staring into space, ignoring her.

'Angie, does Jinty always sing?'

'Always. No, sometimes we sit and just look into each other's eyes for ages. We don't sing then. I just stroke her hands or feet. I'll have to do it tonight, you've got her all excited. Don't worry though, it's lovely.'

Mark reaches across and takes one of Jinty's hands in his. She looks sad to him. He wonders if his silence has upset her and wants to put it right.

Still looking at Jinty, he asks, 'Angie, does Jinty ever make a keening sound… you know, like a seagull? A bit like a scream? On the way here she stopped singing for a while. She looked at a house. She sounded distressed. Frightened.'

Angie pulls a stool to the table and sits. She takes Jinty's other hand. Jinty smiles and looks from her to Mark and back again.

'Mark, Jinty never looks out of windows. She never looks at *things,* only people, or stares into space. I've never heard her scream. What's this about?'

'Sorry I freaked you out. I can't explain. Telling you could drop me in the deepest shit. Something terrible just happened in Kissinger Road.'

'Can I have that chair?' Angie asks. 'It's the one Jinty and me sit in. I don't like her sitting alone really. She's always in my lap.'

'Of course.' Mark rises.

Angie picks Jinty up from the wooden highchair and sits. With practised ease, she reaches behind her and takes two drumsticks from beside the toaster. Crumbs skitter to the floor.

'Drumsticks, of course.' Mark chuckles.

'You should see all around our bed. Castanets, tambourines… I've got a full drum kit.'

'You sleep with Jinty? Sorry, that was personal.'

'Of course I sleep with Jinty. That way I can tell when she needs to go to the toilet. They keep wanting to put a catheter in and she hates that.' She kisses the back of Jinty's head and adds, 'Anyway, she's she best cuddle in the world, aren't you Jinty-Jint?'

Supporting Jinty's head between her breasts, Angie uses the drumsticks to tap a rhythm on the edge of the table. Jinty's hands rise but don't follow the beat. Angie changes the speed and rhythm. Jinty's hands synchronise. She rocks and hums repeated strings of notes. Angie joins in.

Her eyes flick to Mark. 'You not joining in this time?'

'Crikey, no. That's too complicated. I'm only a beginner. How old is Jinty? If it's all right to ask.'

'Eleven. They say she won't get much bigger. You'll stay the perfect dinky Jinty size, won't you, my love? You know, Mark, you're the only person I know who's ever sang with her like you did just now. Were you doing it in the car? Is that why she was so happy? She can't take her eyes off you.'

Mark forms his hands like Jinty's and tries to follow the music.

'Can I get you whatever it is you want from that cupboard?' Mark asks and wishes he hadn't. At once, Angie closes up, hunching slightly: defensive.

Mark rises from the stool. 'Sorry, did I say something wrong? It's just you keep looking at it.' He shoves his hands in his pockets. 'I'd better get going; I've a long walk ahead of me. There's no way I can get my car through all that wreckage. It's bad enough with just the snow.'

He looks back at Angie. 'Is something else wrong?' He waits, seeing some conflict in her, like maybe she's sad he's leaving. He wonders if she gets lonely. 'I'm in no hurry.'

'Can you hang on a minute, then? You'd be doing me a huge favour. The fan's not going to work without electricity.'

'Sorry?' Mark asks.

'I don't smoke near Jinty—well, I do, but only with the fan on and it's been a shit day,' Angie replied.

'Here, Jinty can give me a singing lesson while you nip out. You can keep an eye on me through the window.'

Angie passes her over. Jinty squeaks with delight. Angie stands, pushes strands of hair back, hesitating, like she's not sure about something, and walks to the cupboard.

'I'm going to roll a bloody great joint. Promise you won't tell anyone,' Angie says with her back to Mark.

'Angie, that would drop *you* in the deepest shit. I'm not going to say anything to anyone, ever. And stop looking so tense. Chill out.'

Jinty's thoughtful expression turns to a smile. She stares into Mark's eyes, her head tipping from side to side. Mark tips his too. Jinty changes direction, Mark tries to follow, but Jinty keeps ahead of him, always changing rhythm and speed until Mark splutters, laughing. Jinty squeals with delight. Mark looks up at Angie. She smiles and shakes her head.

'You'll never win at Jinty's games, mister. You've really clicked with her. Won't be a sec.' Angie opens the kitchen door and cries out as snow and wind blast in. The candles blow out. Angie forces the door closed. 'Fuck.' She flicks her lighter and relights a candle. 'I'll smoke in the hall.'

When she returns, the acrid scent of skunk wafts into the kitchen. 'Oh my God, I should've eaten something first.'

Mark gives up trying to tap a complicated beat on the kitchen table. 'Damn, I used to be good at that, but I'm disappointing Jinty–I can't get it accurate enough.'

Angie laughs. 'I've got metronomes that aren't accurate enough for Jinty. Anyway, look at her expression. Does that look like disappointment to you?'

She walks to the hob. 'Tea, coffee, chocolate…? Look… you're going nowhere tonight. I just looked out the front door. It's coming down harder and the wind is really bad. I'd feel like shit making you go.'

'And I was feeling very uncomfortable about going but didn't want to ask. I think I'd be in trouble out there.'

'I'll make you another chocolate. What do you do anyway? You sound really posh but you look a bit scruffy.,'

Jinty stops tapping, her intense eyes flicking to whoever speaks.

'I don't do much at the moment. I… my wife and son were killed in a collision… car crash, two years ago. I didn't handle it well. I took sick leave.' He sighs. 'Life is shit. What do you do?'

Angie hunches slightly. 'Confidential. I'm so sorry about your wife and kid. I sort of know how you feel. I'd be nothing without Jinty.' She hunches a bit more, her arms frozen in the act of lifting the kettle. 'Fuck, I'm nothing much as it is. A hooker… A call-up tart for a bunch of fat, slimy executives in a bank.' She sniffs and swears. 'Shit. Sorry, I don't even know why I dumped that on you. Too much dope probably. You didn't deserve that.'

Jinty mews with pleasure and looks from Angie to Mark.

'Angie,' Mark whispers and rises. 'Here, take Jinty. I'll make the chocolate. Look, for what it's worth, you're a good mother…'

Jinty reaches out for Angie and snuggles in to her as Mark passes her over. His heart breaks for Angie as she looks at him with wet eyes and says, 'Yes… I am. Oh, Jinty needs the loo. Back in a minute.'

Mark finishes making the chocolate and sits at the table. He feels the desolation within him has radiated out into the world, freezing it dead… and then returned, invading the kitchen and clawing back into his soul. When Angie enters, the room warms to Jinty's smile.

Angie looks at Mark and says, 'That's the effect she has on me too. You need a Jinty.'

Mark closes his eyes and sighs. 'Angie, that makes more sense than everything the shrinks have been telling me all year.' He jumps as his phone rings. He listens and says, 'Yes, I'm still here, in one of the flats. You have it clear? How? Jesus, they shifted all the wreckage? Yes, I can do that. I'll meet you at the road in half an hour.'

Rising from his seat, he taps a little rhythm on Jinty's nose. 'I've got to go, you two. The army's here with personnel carriers. The road is clear and I'm to knock on every front door in this section and see if anyone needs help. Do you know any elderly, or vulnerable people, Angie?' He moves to the kitchen door. His leather wallet creaks as he opens it. 'Here, take my card. Phone me if ever you need anything.' He looks into Angie's eyes. 'Can I come and see Jinty again sometime?'

But Angie, scanning the card, asks, 'You a doctor then?'

'A doctor of forensics. I'm… was on the force.'

'A cop… Christ, after all that I told you…'

Mark takes Angie's shoulders. 'Angie, you're both completely safe with me. I promise.'

* * * *

Mark writhes in his bed, turns over and pushes the empty whiskey bottle aside to see the clock. One pm. He'll phone Angie today. He wants to see Jinty, take them both somewhere, perhaps. He'll tidy his house, make a decision about returning to work, speak to his lawyer, clean the kitchen, wash some clothes, open some of the piles of letters… No, he isn't going to do any of that. He rolls over, pulls the duvet close. Pretending it's his wife, Sheila.

Mark's bladder at bursting and his mouth, dry like corundum powder, force him out of bed. No food in the house. Water for breakfast; Mark longs for water. It will be hours before his alcohol-ravaged face can be shown to the world. 'Well,'—his thoughts follow their usual morning routine—'I could drive to where people don't recognise me…' But he can't trust himself to drive. Killing pedestrians lies outside his limits.

He sips handfuls of water from the kitchen tap. He wonders if he pissed in the sink last night. Not that it matters.

His phone vibrates, humming on the table.

'Hi Mark.' Monica's voice again. 'Can you come in, just for an hour or two? We have a serial killer…'

'Monica, please, I have nothing to give you.' He cuts the connection and lays his head on the table.

The kitchen fills with echoes: Sheila, folding washing and chatting, or passing him plates to wash. His son drawing at the table and making the sounds of whatever he draws. Now things lie in stinking piles. Peeling paint, a newspaper yellowed by two years of sun through a dirty window. Mark looks into his aching emptiness, can't even find hope, drinks more water, weeps and falls asleep.

* * * *

Hunger forces him awake, forces him into his car. Slush and meltwater hiss under his tyres as he drives to the supermarket. There's Angie pushing Jinty through the car park. Mark scrambles out, banging his door against another car.

'Hey, Jinty, Angie.' He waves and splashes through puddles. He squats down in front of the grinning Jinty, only her eyes and mouth visible between a fluffy hat and scarf. 'Hey, nice to see you.' He looks up at Angie. 'Can I buy you lunch?'

'Sorry, Mark, I'm in a rush.' She drops her eyes.

'What's the rush? Lunch would be cool.'

'I've got to go…' She catches her breath.

'Can I give you a lift then?'

'No. I'm taking Jinty to a child-minder.' She turns her head away, eyes moist.

A twisting pain shoots through Mark's heart. 'You're going to work?'

'Mark, I've got to go.' Angie starts to push the wheelchair around him.

'Angie… do you have to?'

She doesn't meet his eyes. 'I can't live on benefits. I need to get away from those flats and all the bastards that shout "alien" when they see Jinty.'

'But…'

'Mark, I have to go.' Angie pushes past him.

'Look, Angie, I have a house too big for me. It's a mess at the moment, but…'

'See you later, Mark.'

'Wait… my sick pay is crap, but I could try going back to work, then you could just look after Jinty.'

He stands impotent and tortured. Watches her disappear into the crowd of shoppers. She doesn't look back, the vapour of warm breath twisting around her scarf.

* * * *

'Yes?' Mark says into his phone. He can't remember pressing 'answer' let alone waking up. Two bags of shopping and three bottles of whiskey clutter the kitchen table. He sits up.

'Hi, it's me–Angie. I'm on the bus with Jinty. Remember those noises you said she made–like a seagull? We've just passed the, uh, you know, the bit after the railway station. Jinty is weird, frightened, like she's hurt…'

Mark's heart surges into a pounding rhythm. His chair falls backwards. He grabs his jacket and leaves the front door swinging. 'Get off at the next stop. Go back to the station—go into a shop or something to keep warm. Keep talking, don't switch your phone off.'

'I haven't got much credit…'

'Right, someone will phone you in a minute on a secure line and I'll tap in shortly. You won't need credit.' Mark throws a jacket into the passenger seat of his car. Snow, mud and slush fly from the tyres. He punches through menus and docks his phone.

'Steve? Get Monica to phone this number. Got a pen? No, forget all that, arse. Drop everything. Get to the railway station. Get Monica to tap me into her call. Fuck these traffic lights. Tap me in, someone! Put this call over the speakers. Monica are you there? No, I can't bloody wait. Monica, this is Angie. Angie, Monica's a colleague of mine. I'll be at the station in less than a minute. I'll meet you at the entrance. You'll hear my horn.'

The Land Rover's traction control struggles with Mark's cornering. He presses down on the horn to keep it blaring. Through its pedestrian-scattering noise, he hears Angie from his phone.

'Is that you, Mark? I can hear you coming.'

Mark slows and stops in the middle of the road. Angie's boots struggle to grip. She's carrying Jinty, and clambers in as the passenger door swings open. Mark throws his jacket into the back and runs to get the wheelchair from the pavement.

Jinty looks pale and moans. Mark smiles and ruffles her hair as Angie closes the door. Horns blare behind them.

'God, Mark. You look awful.'

'Hello, Angie. Which way?'

'Back that way.'

Mark's U-turn intensifies the din of protesting drivers. The Land Rover surges forwards.

'Jinty isn't wearing a seat belt. Slow down. She's looking that way,' Angie shouts.

Jinty wails and looks down a side street.

'I'll take the next one,' Mark says, slowing the car a fraction and sliding into the next left turn.

'Left again, Mark. What's happening? Can we get Jinty away from here? Mark, she's looking at that house.'

Mark brakes and crashes the door open. He grabs his phone.

'Melbourne Grove, everyone. Can you drive, Angie?'

'Yes, but…'

'Get out of here. See you at your place.'

As Angie, looking apprehensive, slips into the driving seat, Mark says, 'See you soon,' and squeezes her arm. Jinty keens.

Mark drops the hatch at the back of the car and scrabbles through a holdall. Grabbing a crowbar, he slams the hatch closed and runs to the house.

'Number 26, I'm going to force entry,' he says into his phone. 'Several sets of footprints, very recent, leading in and out. Mine are about a metre to the left.'

The Land Rover pulls away.

The front door of the house stands wide open. A torn blouse lies near the top of the stairs. Mark hears sirens from the road. He storms up the stairs three at a time and stops at the landing.

There's a noise detectable over his panting breath, a scratching behind the half open door ahead. He checks the floor, steps forwards, pushes the handle. A faint click from somewhere.

The naked woman, spread-eagled with her hands and feet nailed to the floor, arches her neck to look at him. The tube taped into her mouth leads to a hole through the carpet. She makes eye-contact with Mark, stiffens and writhes. Her chest and abdomen swell like an inflating life raft. Skin turning blue and shiny. Things moving behind it. A dull explosion and red mist blow Mark backwards.

* * * *

'He's unconscious. I've got him. Go on up,' a man's voice says. Someone feels Mark's ribs, running their hands over his arms and legs, his head and neck. The hand lifts him a little; another runs down his spine.

Mark opens his eyes. Shouting and swearing come from the landing above, voices he knows from work.

'Steve, help me up off these stairs. We've got a job to do.'

'Is this you back in the driving seat, boss?'

'Christ knows… I just saw a woman explode… What the hell's going on?'

* * * *

'Keep the office, Shamus. I don't need it. I want to be right in the centre of things.' Mark looks round the room cluttered with cabinets, chairs and piles of paper. 'Christ, was it always this small?'

Monica, tall, slim, forties, blue skirt-suit, laughs. 'Were you always this scruffy?'

'These are the best clothes I could find in the pile.'

'Why are you here, Mark? Why now? We've asked often enough.' Monica tilts her head on one side and points a pen at him.

He pauses, shrugs. 'I met an angel…or two.' His fists clench, mouth hardens. 'I looked into that woman's eyes as she died. I killed her, didn't I? That was set up.'

Shamus says, 'Set up all right. We were tipped off a few minutes after you called us. The team is there now. Two huge gas cylinders in the room below. A tube for her mouth and another…'

Mark waves everyone quiet. 'Where are we?'

The door opens and a man in his thirties, casually dressed, walks in. 'Hi, gang,' he says, and waves. 'Mark, the Chief wants to see you.'

'She'll have to wait, Steve. Thanks for rescuing me. You freshened up?'

'That suit goes in the bin, can't stand blood. You called a meeting?'

'Tell me everything,' Mark says.

'A drug dealer, cocaine mostly, forced into half-solidified cement. A young woman's body hanging over a rope–her back snapped in half. Beside her, a woman blown to pieces by a large firework up her rectum and now a woman… well, you saw. All over the last five days.'

Mark waved his hand. 'What connections?'

'Nothing much. No real pattern apart from…' Monica pauses.

Shamus chips in, '…the way that everything has taken some imagination and a great deal of effort. Spontaneity is out. Planning and preparation are in. We're overwhelmed and so are the labs. Info is coming in too slowly… and people are dying.'

Mark holds hands up for silence. 'Then we solve this before anyone else dies. Monica, that programme is rubbish in emergencies. It needs too much information and it sounds like we don't have much. Steve, we need every flipchart in this building. We're going to do this by steam. No time for knocking on doors. Phone, pen and flipchart only. Shamus, get the files on each victim.'

Steve hesitates. 'I'm not taking my wife out tonight?'

'Sorry, Steve. You're marrying us for the foreseeable future. Now, where were we? And why are people standing still?'

Monica lifts a phone. 'When did you last eat a meal, Mark?'

Mark shrugs.

'Will pizza do you?'

The door opens again and silence falls. Mark turns to the woman entering. Stark suit, stark face: a driven face, a person who doesn't see the need to camouflage greying hair.

She looks Mark up and down. 'Hello, Mohammed–the mountain just came to you.' She lifts a hand as Mark's mouth opens. 'Don't say anything unless it's a convincing explanation of how you knew where and when Elizabeth Greyfriar was going to die. You killed her: you are a suspect until I know more.' The hand waivers, the expression softens. 'But don't let that stop you here.'

Monica picks up a file. 'Here's the file on the prostitute, Michelle, take a look. I've included Mark's explanation about the allegedly psychic girl.'

The Chief Inspector takes it. 'What are your conclusions, Monica?'

Monica shrugs. 'What damage would it do to my career if I said that I hadn't totally written it off as nonsense?'

* * * *

Mark throws a cold and dry pizza crust in the direction of a bin. 'I think I've worn the phone out. What have you got, Shamus?'

Shamus turns from his flipchart. 'Too many little things and nothing very much. Rather than read everything out, can I suggest we look at each other's charts?'

Mark shrugs. 'Fine, let's do that.' The heavy mug of tea in his hand empties in sips until he's finished reading each chart. He sits on his desk until everyone has finished studying each other's notes. 'Well, Monica?'

'Too little… I'd say money.'

'Shamus?' Mark says.

'I'm with Monica: money.'

'Steve?'

'A person or persons that want us to work out what they are trying to say so we deliver their message to the media… money.'

Mark nods. 'Yes, we're all together on that one. I've not done a serial before, but it looks like a grudge.' He walks to his flipchart and turns the first sheet over. 'New page. "Money". And don't worry about the phone bill.'

Mark doesn't like inconveniencing people, but getting property developers and city investors out of bed and interrogating them over the phone at four o'clock in the morning doesn't feel as wrong as disturbing a nurse or van driver. He wonders why.

'Christ, I'm beginning to stink,' he says at six-thirty am. 'Come on, flipchart-scrutinising time again. I'm sorry. No one goes home if they can possibly remain here.'

Monica sweeps back tangled hair. 'You do stink, I look like an earthquake victim, and Shamus almost has a crease in his shirt.' She looks at the last chart and circles some words with a highlighter. 'No one goes home for any reason at all. So, the only thing the victims have in common is a connection with the bank, BTB—I take it, Steve, that BTB means Ballings, Thompson, and Blakelock? So… they meet once a year as a Board, very nice, very tricky to find. Very well done, us.'

Steve throws a pencil at the chart. 'What the hell are we going to do? Do we contact every person that's ever supplied a BTB board member with cocaine or rented them facilities for banquets, or who's a board member's toyboy or mistress set up in a luxury love nest paid for by the bank? That's what we've got here, isn't it? Not the board members themselves, just people associated with them.'

'We could protect the board. We can't protect the thousands of people with whom they may have been in contact. Hey, look at this: BTB announced losses *and* huge bonuses last week. Someone is pissed off with them.'

'That would be a *lot* of people,' Shamus says. 'Maybe thousands of investors. How are we going to sift through that lot in a hurry?'

'I'm knackered and not thinking straight,' Mark says and slumps in a chair. 'Ideas please. Hang on, that's mine.' He pulls his phone out, fumbles and drops it. It falls apart on the floor. 'Shit.'

He picks up the pieces, slides the battery in and snaps the back on. 'Bollocks, it's dead. I didn't recognise the number. Why didn't I recognise the number? No one calls this unless I know them.'

'SHIT!' His palms hit the desk and papers fly to the floor.

'Right. No questions. Do as I say. Steve, we need weapons; get them now, *NOW!* Shamus, hit panic–I need every officer. Get them to this area.' A plastic chair crashes against a waste bin as he runs to the wall-map. His pen squeaks a line round the Beeches Estate. 'I want it sealed so that not even a fly can get in or out…'

'Jinty!' Monica cries.

Shamus interrupts, 'Not a hope in hell, we don't have that sort of manpower any more. Things have changed.'

Mark's brain crashes. He freezes and splutters. Neurons fire in new directions. 'Shamus, the army's still here: do it.'

Monica says, 'I'll do comms. Radios, everyone check in.'

'What's going on, Mark?' Shamus asks, punching numbers into a desk phone.

'Jinty must be crying. I'm going there now. Where the *fuck* is Steve?'

* * * *

Mark drives the Land Rover over the curb hidden under a drift. The car rises and crashes down on frozen turf. Shards of plastic bumper bounce and spin into snow. Sliding in slush, grass and mud, Mark slams his foot on the brake.

The car skids out of control. He opens the door and prepares to release his seat belt. The car hits a tree and bolts explode as the door rips off. Mark, already out, pounds for the stairs and the walkway that lead to Angie and Jinty.

Steve scrambles after him, pistol in hand. Mark races into the flat— the door wide open. No one there. Still warm; people must have left only moments ago. Rubber bungees all over the hall floor. Mark yells for Angie.

A hand on his shoulder. He whirls round. It's Steve. Mark rushes out, leaning over the walkway parapet screaming for Angie and Jinty.

His world whirls around a tiny dot.

Jinty.

Jinty and her beaming smile, her teasing eyes, the way she makes you forget about anything but you and her.

Streaming hot tears, dry, hoarse throat from shouting. Not thinking straight, not following tracks in the snow. Random dashes to possible hiding places, or places where bodies could be dumped. Bleeding hands from wrenching open icy bins and bags. People stare from a hundred windows that reflect flashing blue and red lights.

A woman's voice calling from a balcony.

Mark's still running, sliding, looking into shadows under bushes, kicking open a bicycle shed, running, running. Steve grabbing him. Stopping him. Shouting at him, shaking his shoulders, mouthing words again and again, until they break through fathoms of panic and despair.

'Three arrests, two suspects holed up... the army.... A woman and handicapped girl... matching the description... hiding with neighbours... listen, you arse. Mark, *Mark! They're safe.*'

Angie running towards him, snow bursting up around her boots.

CHUG-A-MONKEY

STEPHEN GODDEN

'ON THE RAGA, BRUV,' DCR SAID. 'Big old engine block in front of me. Blew it away, pulse-boomed that mother to oblivation, cross the nation, dime out time and break the face-man.'

Slamma winced. 'Shit, blood, don't go throwing down rhymes, you ain't got the slam.'

DCR blushed and hunched down to hide his embarrassment, staring at the plate of chips and pizza in front of him. Soul food, Slamma called it. DCR preferred eggs, bacon and sausages with his chips, but Slamma said that was old man food. Pizza was what the blood ate. DCR wanted to be blood, wanted his skin inked. Slamma had an AK tatted cross his shoulders—just like in GTA—showed up dark black against his pale skin. He shaved his head bald. Coz the blood did, he said. DCR's younger sister said it was coz he was ginger.

The college cafeteria was pretty busy. Tuesday was curry day, but Slamma, DCR, and the other TrueBlood crew ate their pizza and sneered at the curry-heads. Not too openly, mind, because some of them mofos were bad. Called the TrueBloods geeky wigga mopheads and nobody done nothing to stop'em dissing. DCR wanted to, but Slamma said it weren't the right time.

DCR brushed a stray lock of dark hair out of his grey-blue eyes. He kept his hair long, like Conan. Had to regain ground here, get his pride back, so he said, 'Should have seen it go boom, stunnifaction city, bruv.'

'Where this block at?' Slamma said around a mouthful of pizza.

DCR wiped the crumbs and spittle from his face. 'You know, drop down the manhole, crawl, swim through the sewer, up by the old palace. On the greenback hill.'

'Whoa bro, big old purple block, with grey strips, designate 42 on the side?'

'Yeah that the one, killed a mofo lot of spider-clones after.'

'Shit-stain refrain, that block your block.'

'What you say?'

'That block your upgrade, bruv, take your ship up to destroyer class. I riffed it out for you, blood, told you look out for 42. Reason you in that city is to get that block. And you blew it up. Stunastic.' Slamma started laughing. 'Yo, SlipLock,' he called across the aisle to the gangling Asian with a triple line of dumbbells through his eyebrow. 'DCR blew the 42 block.'

SlipLock started laughing. 'You mad, bruv, broke the game, gotta go back and try that shit again.'

'Sweet rhyme,' Slamma said. 'Spinning out, all in flame, got no-one but yourself to blame, broke the game, spun the flame, lost the time in the last refrain.'

'Sweet.' SlipLock nodded his head to some internal rhythm. 'You know it, you know it, oh. You know it, you know it, oh.'

Slamma joined into the call and response. Nobody else in the cafeteria did.

DCR glanced around. He wished he could be cool like Slamma and SlipLock, they didn't give a fuck. Throwing down their rhymes right there in the cafeteria. In front of all the college. They didn't care that the haters were laughing over on their table by the wall.

'Boom krakaboom.' Slamma slapped out a three-beat on the table that made his coffee fall into his lap. 'Ow, fuck, fuck.'

'You done boiled your dick, blood,' somebody called out. 'You know it, you know it, oh. You know it, you know it, oh.'

Everybody joined in the call and response.

* * * *

Slamma had washed down his baggy jeans in the toilet but the top of his Calvins was stained bad above the low-riding denim. So he pulled the long hoody out of his locker and put it on, despite the heat. Wore his dark shades to class too, till Mr Simmonds told him to take them off.

'This is art appreciation, Mr Reynolds. You can't appreciate art if you can't see it.'

Slamma mumbled that his name was Slamma.

'Yes, Timothy, I'm sure that it is.'

DCR always sat at the front of the class for art. Slamma said to take the course coz it was easy credits, but DCR took a drawing class too and he wanted to take a few more next term. Slamma sneered at art, he was taking music. Though he couldn't actually play an instrument, he said his rhymes and spinning would get him in. DCR wasn't sure about that. Spinning and scratching on BustaGangster discFreak weren't the same as actually doing it for real; you just hit buttons on BGF.

They sat back in the cafeteria drinking coke and eating more pizza. DCR had marinara this time, coz he was tired of the meatfeast.

Slamma shook his head. 'Wanna be blood and don't like the meat.'

DCR looked down at the table.

'So you gotta go back to your dime before the sewer, do that shit over. Kill the mofo spider-clones then lift up the block and take it back to your ship. Gotta watch your hud though, your immersion suit needs full power to lift that mofo.'

'But I'm spinning off a single dime,' DCR said. 'Can't go back, ain't got a save. Saved it after the spider-clones.'

'Spinning off a single…shit, blood, this ain't no fracking shooter spree game. This is a slipslide RPG. You gotta use all your dimes. Spinning off a single dime. Mofo retard, you restart toasty, bruv.'

'I've got forty hours game time in. I can't go back to restart.'

'You gotta, blood, just gotta. Ain't no other way.'

'I know a way,' a soft contralto voice said. The two boys looked around. Ellen Genesric stood next to the table. Her long blonde hair flowed down her back like a wave of silk, a short red skirt showed off her naked legs and the black Metallica tour tee was artfully ripped to reveal smooth, tanned flesh.

Slamma said nothing, so DCR said, 'Hi, Merc.' Everybody called Ellen Mercedes, because she was one fine ride.

Her stunning blue eyes flashed dangerously for a moment. 'Hello, David.'

DCR said, 'I'm called DCR.'

'And I'm called Ellen.'

'Oh.' David mumbled a sorry.

Ellen tossed her head, the sunlight gleamed from her hair and David felt the tension crawl across his skin like an electrostatic shawl. 'It's okay, DCR, you didn't know I dropped that name. Though Merc is nice, better than Mercedes, like a mercenary isn't it.' She smiled and her tongue flicked briefly across her teeth.

DCR's throat clamped shut but he managed to stutter, 'You know a way to get me a destroyer?'

'Better, I know a way to get you a cruiser.'

'No fucking way, ho!' Slamma exclaimed.

'You calling my sister a ho?' Ellen's brother Jack started to lift his fourteen stone of raw muscle out of his seat.

Slamma got even paler. DCR tensed, ready to protect his friend. Jack weren't much bigger than DCR. He'd get a few licks in.

'Did I ask you to stand up for me?' Ellen snapped at her brother.

'Hey.' Jack sat down. 'You want to hang with the freak squad that's your deal.' He lifted his hands to his side, but the moment Ellen turned back to face DCR he wagged a warning finger at Slamma and gave a big grin that did not reach his eyes.

Slamma looked away and DCR didn't blame him. Jack was into kick-boxing.

'Do you mind if I sit down?' Ellen didn't wait for an answer and sat right next to DCR. So close her knee touched his briefly. 'There's another engine block over the other side of the city, hidden under that pyramid.'

'You can't spike that pyramid, no way in,' Slamma said.

'I know a way.' Ellen glanced at Slamma. He was staring at her tits. She sniffed and turned back to DCR. Who was very careful to keep his gaze fixed on her face. 'I can show you if you like.'

'You can?'

'Yeah, I'll come over to yours. Tonight all right?'

'Er…Yeah, I live—'

'I know where you live.' Ellen smiled again and stood up, putting a hand on his shoulder. 'About seven okay?'

'Y…yes.'

'I'll look forward to it.' Ellen smiled again.

Slamma watched her arse as she walked away. Then, with a quick glance at Jack, leaned in and whispered to DCR, 'That bitch wants me so bad.'

* * * *

Slamma came over to DCR's that evening. He was wearing his best stuff, the bleached white denims riding low, with black Calvins, the pink wife-beater to show off his tats, bulky gold chain around his neck, NYC cap turned back and knock-off Chanel shades. His new fake Rolex made the fat on his forearm pinch up a bit, but he could get another link put in.

He swaggered into DCR's crib: a small granny flat on the back of his parent's house. They had let him move in there when he turned sixteen. His father had smiled and said, 'The boy needs some space.' Slamma looked around the small living room with the old cathode telly in the corner wired up to DCR's console, the banging stereo with the racked CDs above (all rap stuff; DCR kept his rock albums in a box under his bed), and the weight bench off to the side with DCR's jacket slung over it.

'Mercedes not here, yet?' Slamma asked.

'Nah,' DCR said. He doubted she would turn up at all, probably just playing a joke on them.

'Knew that mofo bitch would play it cool and turn up late. Make me sweat some.'

DCR glanced at the clock. It was just gone six forty-five. 'She said seven, bruv.'

'Yeah, like I said, late.' Slamma sprawled on the sofa, which was really a little large for the room; DCR's parents had brought it in here when they bought a new suite for the house. A matching armchair under the window was the only other furniture in the room. 'I'm gonna fuck her hard, blood. Make her squeal like a pink machine.'

DCR didn't like him talking that way about Ellen, but he only said, 'She doesn't know you're gonna be here, bruv.'

'Course she does. She knows we hang. It's just clever bitch shit, so that mofo brother of hers don't get wind. She sat across from me, blood, damn near flashed her tits right in my face. That means she wants me. She wants a taste of the slam-dunk express. You know it, bruv.'

DCR remembered the touch of Ellen's knee against his and said nothing.

'What tunes you got?' Slamma got up, walked over to the stereo and rummaged around until he found *Jigglechains, Baby* by the Treadstone crew.

Ellen turned up at precisely seven o'clock. 'Turn that shit off.'

* * * *

'See.' Ellen blasted her way past the last acid-snake clone and used her mag gun to open the last seal on the pyramid.

'Cruiser engine block is just through there.'

'You play good for a bitch,' Slamma said from the armchair under the window. Ellen had said there wasn't enough room for three on the large sofa, then sat very close to DCR.

Ellen shook her head and sighed. 'I'm hungry.'

Slamma leaned forward. 'Yeah, I know what—'

'I want ice-cream.'

'Ice-cream?' DCR shrugged. 'I've got some—'

'Do you have Chug-a-Monkey flavour?'

'Ain't nobody like that Chug-a-Monkey,' Slamma said. 'It tastes like old socks.'

'I like it,' Ellen said. She turned back to DCR. 'Come on. I showed you how to get a cruiser. Get me some ice-cream, please.'

Slamma grinned slowly. 'Yeah, you go and get us some ice-cream, blood.'

'Yeah, okay.' DCR stood up and looked for his wallet.

'Slamma can go,' Ellen said suddenly. 'He's got his car with him. Have to go right over to Waitrose to get Chug-a-Monkey flavour. That's on the other side of town.'

DCR was confused. 'I don't mi—'

'Yeah, Slamma can go.' Ellen looked at Slamma from under lowered eyelashes. 'Please, will you... I'm desperate. I'll be very grateful.'

'Yeah, sure, babe.' Slamma leapt to his feet.

Ellen whispered something in Slamma's ear just before she closed the door behind him. DCR told himself he didn't care.

'You got any other music besides this rap shit?' Ellen asked. 'Oh never mind.' She connected her iPod to the stereo and set the volume to low as Marvin Gaye started to sing about sexual healing.

DCR, quite suddenly, found it quite hard to breathe, because Ellen had started dancing slowly to the music. She held out her hands to him. He looked up at her stupidly. She sighed, sashayed over to him and pulled him to his feet.

'Dance with me.'

She flowed into his arms, the whole length of her body moulded to his. Warm, soft, womanly flesh, pressed tight against DCR. Her thigh slipped between his, her other thigh around his leg, her…

DCR pulled away. 'Look, this is some sort of joke right? Some sort of bet?'

Ellen smiled sadly. 'You poor idiot. Come here.' She led him over to the mirror and stood next to him. 'Look at me.'

DCR looked into the reflection of her eyes.

She asked, 'What do you see?'

DCR spoke the truth. 'You're beautiful.'

'And that is what I see when I look at you.' Ellen kissed him softly on the cheek and slipped back inside the circle of his arms. 'Two months playing that bloody game in the hope that you would notice and I still had to come up and talk to you first. Shit, I talked about the damn game so loudly my friends think I'm freaking crazy.'

'Slamma will be back soon,' DCR said.

'No he won't.' Ellen kissed her way up DCR's neck. 'I told him to sod off out of it. In words he would understand.' Then just before she began to nibble at his earlobe, Ellen whispered, 'Stop thinking.'

So he did.

Vox Vocis

Girdharry

I T STARTED ON MONDAY: AN itch on her skin, right in the
middle of her back, demanding to be scratched. Mandy squirmed
against the typing chair. As she rubbed on the upholstery, saliva
of pleasure wetted her mouth. Each time she stopped wriggling, the
irritation returned. From close by came the tiniest laugh of mockery:
'Ha, ha.'

Goosebumps ran along her arms. She risked a quick glance around
to check that the others were busy at their consoles, then lifted the
paperweight; nothing under there. She rifled through the waste paper
bin; still nothing. She must've been longer than she intended with the
papers, probably shouldn't have tipped them out on the floor, because
David, the office manager, came to her desk.

'Is everything alright, Mandy?'

'Yes, I've... mislaid something.'

'Well, let me know if I can help.' He stood there, frowning and
pursing his lips. So she smiled, just to convince him she was perfectly
fine.

'Ha, ha, ha.'

Now it seemed to come from under David's shoes. She knew he
couldn't hear it, no one else ever could. She forced herself to continue
looking at his face. After he left, she ignored the dread churning her
insides and stuffed the papers back in the bin.

In her experience, it was best to act normally; after all, she didn't want
to arouse suspicion. Taking her purse from the desk drawer, she left the
office and pushed through the silver swing doors into the corridor.

Past the flick-flack of the giant photocopier, she arrived at the vending
machine. Her coins clinked in, followed by a thud as the black-and-

gold-wrapped bar tumbled down. She tore the wrapper, inhaling the sweet chocolate scent before biting. The sticky delight dissolved in her mouth, coating her teeth. *What about those extra calories?* No worries, she'd skip lunch to compensate. As the last of the caramel melted away, she rubbed the silky blouse at her back.

'Ha, ha.'

An unmistakable sneer. She glanced up and down the corridor; empty. With her hands pressed to her temples, she squeezed to keep the panic inside. *Think. Ah yes. Washing, sometimes, washing helps.*

In the Ladies, she soaped her hands and rinsed them, three times in a row. Somewhere in the middle of it a girl came in. Mandy avoided her curious gaze and after the girl left, took one more squeeze of pink gel and a final rinse.

Thanks to her long years in the company, she had pole position next to the window. Despite the view over the car park, the office atmosphere stifled her that afternoon; the air dry, lifeless. She writhed on her royal blue seat, which gave no comfort. Concentration eluded her, the itch scrabbling at her back. The more she scratched, the bolder grew the laughter, until it sounded right behind her. She spun her chair around and stared into empty space.

David looked up from his desk, brown eyes of concern focused in her direction. Heat flushed her cheeks. A few minutes later, under the excuse of a headache, she took flexi-time and scurried home.

A nice hot shower, that's what I need. Afterwards, she pushed aside Joe's shaving gel and smeared the cold of the mirror, clearing an arc of mist. The ceiling spot lights left no place to hide the bulge of tummy fat. *Oh well, just pretend it's not there.*

She bent her arm to grate at her back. After a few seconds, her flaccid muscles gave up, unable to sustain the contortion. So she turned sideways, twisting to get a view. Ah yes, right there, a patch of raspberry red against white skin, just in the small of her back. She grabbed the hairbrush, scraped it back and forth.

'Ha, ha, ha.'

The unpleasant tones bounced off the tiles. Mandy stopped dead, stretched out and grabbed her towelling bathrobe, warm from the rail. She wrapped it around her, fingers fumbling on the thick cotton, at the same time scanning the bathroom, checking up in the corners. She tugged the belt tight into a knot. *Carry on as normal. Don't let it get to you. It's not real.* Clenching the hairbrush handle, its hard plastic digging into her palm, she headed for the bedroom.

She'd stuffed away her experience of being invaded by voices, blanked out the memory of medical scrutiny and medication. She'd been subjected to it for years. They hadn't trusted her then, not after she'd hacked her wrists. She couldn't go back to that, not again. *I can beat this on my own. I know I can.*

All day Tuesday, she wriggled on her blue chair. At intervals, she escaped to the Ladies to scrape the hairbrush over red patch. She fancied she could feel a bump and when she inspected that evening, her suspicion was confirmed. She discovered a lump, barnacle-sized, the skin erupting, ugly. *That's revolting.*

'Ha, ha, ha.'

The derision rang out. She whirled to stand with her back to the mirror, eyes flicking around the bathroom, searching. She knew the voice, understood its strength and the way it could find a way in to bend her mind. She stared at the healed gashes on her wrists; solid evidence of its power. *Don't let it get to you.*

'Leave me alone. Please.'

The orange fish on the shower curtain carried on twisting through the seaweed.

She scuttled to bed to wrap herself in the safety of the duvet, tucking it around her body, making sure she left no spaces. *I'm safe in here. Joe'll be home soon.*

When she'd married Joe, her friend Caz had said, 'Spud you like, spud you marry.' Mandy didn't mind the remark because she saw herself as quite plain, just like her husband and Joe turned out to be loyal and predictable. 'Yes, but does he make you feel good?' Caz asked. Well, he'd never made her feel bad. Is that what she meant? Caz tutted and rolled her eyes.

Despite her reluctance to enter the bathroom on Wednesday morning, nothing strange transpired. She smeared her blue eye shadow with haste. In the background, plates clattered as Joe emptied the dishwasher, tunes playing on the radio. She imagined him spreading marmalade on two slices of toast, everything normal. Maybe she'd be lucky this time.

At work, she kept busy all day with the monthly conference; plugging in electronics, sorting out cables for the young wannabees. Each time she bent, the growth caught on her blouse. She couldn't risk a peek in the Ladies. *What if someone else sees it?* So she carried on, ensuring the coffee and biscuits were wheeled in on time and the jugs stayed topped up with water.

That evening, she discovered a limpet-sized growth, the skin thick, gross; her fingers recoiled. The bathroom swirled. Mandy clutched the side of the sink, closing her eyes as peals of mocking laughter resounded off the misted walls.

For a moment, she contemplated seeing Dr Jameson. The last time she sat in front of his unsmiling face was after her son, Terry, moved to Singapore. Life had seemed so empty. She drifted ghost-like from day to day, wishing he still lived around the corner. The voice knew it, perceiving her weakness. It came to pay a visit, came to twist her will to its own end. She recalled the gashes on Joe's chest after the voice made her attack him. Then Jameson gave her shots, put a stop to it. But she never liked his look, always felt like crawling from his room, useless, hardly worth his time.

Thursday passed and she didn't call him.

'He can't help you.'

She agreed; besides, she remembered how much she hated him, hated his cunning eyes. Good job the voice had reminded her of that.

After work, the lump revealed itself bigger than ever. It squatted on her back, an angry red volcano, hard and scaly.

'You can't escape.'

She pressed hands over her ears and ran from the bathroom.

Curled in bed, perspiration trickled down her temple. She stared at the wallpaper Joe had hung for her years ago, red and pink roses. She picked out where each stem joined a flower across the seam, or where two cut parts came together to form a whole bloom. Under the duvet, she hugged her knees, rocking backwards and forwards, counting off each rose.

Caz's mother had died of cancer. Mandy had seen her once, frail and limp with nausea after a treatment. The cancer had started with a small lump. After a year of bombardment by radiation and chemicals, it lived on.

Mandy closed her eyes to a vision of malignant cells coursing around her own bloodstream.

Friday, she wore a baggy blouse to work, so nobody would notice the bulge.

'Are you OK, Mandy? You seem a bit...distracted,' David said.

'He detests you. He wants to get rid of you.'

She dug her nails into her palms. 'I'm fine, just a bit tired, that's all,' she lied, balanced on a fine point between terror of madness and dread of terminal disease. She tottered through the day, comforted by vending machine confectionary.

When she returned home, the eruption appeared hideous. A fist-sized lump sat on her back, formed of an alien substance, with the skin over the top flaking, vile. It brought her to her knees. The floor pressed against her shins, reminding her of childhood days at the convent school. The laughter derided her, bent her head. Mandy sobbed. The mockery shoved harder, pushing her head to the floor.

'Nowhere to hide, Mandy.'

She crawled out the door, along the beige landing carpet.

Joe came back early, coming into the bedroom. His voice sounded a long way away.

'David called me. I know there's something wrong. We've an appointment with Jameson. Get dressed.'

She gripped the duvet with both hands, but allowed Joe to prise it from her, a small part of her aware that she'd lost the battle.

She entered Jameson's office, the tang of disinfectant sharp in her nostrils.

'Don't trust him. He wants to hurt you.'

'How are you feeling, Mandy?' Jameson leant his elbows on the desk.

She shrugged, avoiding his eyes, staring at his glittering cufflinks.

'Don't tell him anything.'

'I'm a bit run down, that's all. I guess it's my age.'

'Have you been hearing voices?'

The voice came closer. She felt its icy grip on her, its frosty presence against the side of her cheek.

'He's tricking you.'

In the corner of her vision, she could see Joe sitting on the couch, one hand on top of the other in his lap. Dependable Joe; it wrenched her gut to disappoint him again.

'Well, I...'

Jameson steepled his fingers. 'Shall we try some medication? Would that help?'

She nodded, a wave of shame washing over her.

'Don't trust him.'

Saturday morning, she didn't bother getting dressed. Joe laid out her medication on the kitchen table. She eyed it; three purple, elongated capsules, same as the ones she'd pretended to swallow the night before.

'They want to hurt you.'

She took the capsules in her hand, a glass of water in the other. Joe ate his breakfast, watching her every move. She feigned tossing the capsules into her mouth, took a gulp of water. As Joe's gaze flicked to his scrambled eggs, she slipped the capsules into her bathrobe pocket.

Joe hung around the house most of the day, doing odd jobs in the garden. She padded in and out of the kitchen in the fluffy panda slippers her son had bought her, stirring up mugs of hot chocolate, tucking into the biscuits she kept for emergencies.

Everything went well until she decided to call Terry. It should be evening in Singapore. The phone rang and rang. He was probably out having fun with his wife.

'She's turned him against you.'

She pressed the receiver down hard, clenching her teeth.

'He promised he'd keep in touch. See how he lied.'

Joe came into the living room. He raised an eyebrow. 'Was that Terry?'

'No, he's not there.' She gazed into space.

'Get rid of him.'

She took a biscuit. 'Aren't you going down the pub as usual?'

Joe put his hands in his pockets. He shook his head.

'The others will miss you.'

'Perhaps.'

'But it's Saturday. You don't have to worry about me. I'm feeling much better.' She offered him a biscuit, then waited a moment, pitching the tone of her voice for maximum impact. 'Don't you trust me?' She watched him squirm.

'It's not that.'

'Well then? Why not go for an hour or something, I'm really fine.'

'Well...maybe, but not for long. How about watching a film together later?'

She nodded.

When she heard the front door slam, she shuffled into the kitchen to make another hot chocolate, then went back to bed. She took out her romance novel and opened it at the marker, her drink forgotten on the bedside table as she followed sultry Brendon's exploits.

After the crescendo, Mandy swung her legs out of bed and headed downstairs. What made her enter the bathroom, she didn't know; maybe a morbid sense of horror at her own disfigurement. One more look.

The growth throbbed, ugly, taking her over, bit by bit.

'Time to put an end to it, Mandy.'

She looked in the mirror, smiled, her eyes cold. *Yes, what a good idea.*

In the kitchen, she hunted for a knife. Joe had hidden them, but not well enough.

'See how he tries to control you?'

Coming up the stairs, she held the bread knife with the blade pointing down, but in the bathroom she gripped the handle, ready to make a swing.

'Cut it out.'

She turned sideways, lifted the knife behind her, held the blade close to her skin, then brought it down with a chop. It sliced through easily. The burn of the blade drove the voice to a screaming frenzy. *'Yes! Yes!'*

A red glob of flesh splattered to the floor. She stared at it, spittle flecking her lips, tightened her grip, swung again and again. Hacking at the growth, cutting through years of numbness, a lifetime of pushing it all down. Livid gobs hit the tiles. A red river coursed down her back. As she scythed, the agony of the cutting transformed into a sear of ecstasy. She floated out of her own body, watched from above as the gore splattered down. Until at last the knife fell with a clatter from her fingers. The smatterings of flesh stared at her, accusing; depression, broken promises, loneliness.

She shuffled to bed. She'd cut the poison out, got down to the truth. A dark red stain spread across the mattress as she closed her eyes.

My Father's Micrometer

Alf Haywood

AREFUL, BE CAREFUL, I'M NOT used to sunlight anymore, not like I used to be. Opening my box so suddenly, without warning, why anything might have happened! I could have fallen apart with metal fatigue, or rust; those things are quite likely at my age.

How old am I, you ask? Well I suppose I started off as a few scraps of steel just lying about, some time in the thirties; that's the nineteen-thirties to you. Then this young lad, an apprentice he were then, he took those scraps and cut them very accurately to size; well, my size in fact. He filed some and turned others on a lathe; ever so carefully he did it. Then very delicately he added all those measurements you see around my middle. He were careful all right, that lad. I hardly felt a thing all the time he was cutting and scraping; although it did tickle when he started polishing some of me fiddly bits.

The reason he were so precise of course, was because he wanted me to be his special piece. Something so precise and accurate that he would be considered good enough to be an engineer.

I had a brief look at all the things made by the other apprentices and a few of them, to be honest, were quite good; but I was the best. I was smooth and accurate no matter what I had to measure. This meant that between us, we were at last allowed to work full time, making and measuring all manner of complicated bits and pieces.

The best years of all came after that, because we were busy every blessed day—nights as well sometimes—preparing for something called a war. Between that lad and me we made some beautiful machine parts. Beautiful and powerful they were; why, some even flew through the skies with great roars and the ground shook as they passed over.

Before I knew it, that lad were a man full grown, and when men gets to a certain age they start courting. Next thing I know, I'm stuck in that box for a day or three while he has a honeymoon, whatever that is. I mean, I've never fancied getting up close to a set of spanners or the oilcan, but it seemed to make him very happy to have a wife. Too happy at times; that's how I got my first bit of damage, when he spun me right up in the air because he had fathered something or other just as the air raid siren sounded. Of course he soon straightened me out, but I were always a bit nervous of being dropped again after that.

Then it all changed, very sudden like. One day we were as busy as ever and then it were over. They didn't want all those parts we had been making. It might have been a coincidence but I realised shortly afterwards that I never heard that siren wail again.

It was a bit disappointing not to be so busy, but it was fine for a few years until his wife persuaded him to become a grocer instead of an engineer. I didn't really understand what that meant, but I soon found out. When I did, I honestly wished I'd never been made. He put me in a box all on my own, and he put the box in a bag along with every other tool he possessed. We never saw the light of day for twenty-four long dreary years. No tool, no instrument should have to endure that; it were hell on earth with nothing to do but slowly rust away at the bottom of a cupboard.

Some say there's a great machine somewhere that hears all the cries of the lonely instruments and is able to help them back to a useful life. I don't know if that's true, but after all those years of asking for help, the box opened and he needed me again.

It seemed he was fed up being a grocer and wanted to be an engineer once more. So he polished and oiled me as good as new to get me ready for work. Naturally I thought it would be just the same as before; but I was quite mistaken. He had to attend some course, to learn about all the new fangled machines that had been invented while he'd been a grocer; especially something they eventually called a computer. Personally I thought it looked a bit pathetic, just a metal box on the end of the lathe that didn't move.

That course turned out to be quite a bit of fun really. The instructors running it soon had to show a bit of respect to my man when they asked where he bought me. I remember the look of astonishment on their faces as he answered, 'I never bought it, I made it as an apprentice.' They all had a good look at me then, and again when I proved all their special samples were rubbish. Why some of them were wrong by over a thousandth of an inch, more than enough to crash one of our wartime flying things.

It was different after that though. He still kept me in his pocket ready to use, but somehow whatever he made was controlled by that metal box and I was only used to double check just a few of the bits we made. As time went on we made fewer and fewer pieces, until eventually someone suggested that he stopped making anything. After that, we just concentrated on sorting out problems created by other engineers. I think they thought he were very good at his job, but getting a bit too slow, so we carried on just tinkering rather than making; which I enjoyed because it were much more interesting.

Then, in one horrible moment, it ended. It ended when he felt some sort of pain inside his head; his hand lost its grip on me and I started to fall. He had never dropped me after that first accident, but this was much, much worse because this time he fell with me and we both had to wait until somebody came to help us. He must have been damaged a lot more than me; they took him away in a noisy ambulance and whatever they did it was a rubbish repair because he could never hold me properly again.

I saw him only once after that, when he tried to clean me up a little and cover me in oil, 'To keep me safe,' he said. I knew our life together was almost over as he struggled with one hand to complete that simple task. His other hand, the left one, it were clenched up tight in a ball, as if it would never open again. I think that was the only time I ever saw him cry.

A few months later, his wife opened the box and shed a tear or two as she handed me over to another young man saying.

'He would have wanted you to have this.'

He is a nice lad but he's somebody's son, not an engineer. He said he would always look after me and possibly even fix me on a wall or something as a reminder of the man who made me; but like a lot of good intentions, it hasn't happened yet.

I've been in that box ever since, and I was just wondering, are you by any chance an engineer who needs a micrometer?

I Remember

Shuna Meade

THIS IS THE FIRST TIME I've been back in fifty years. Harrisons have been coastguards here for generations—Dad was the last of us. He handed in his notice when the body of a boy was found speared by the rocks we called the Monster's Teeth. No-one was surprised after what had happened to Mum.

'Down the High Street, out to the lighthouse and back, should take you about an hour.' The concierge traces the way on the brochure map he hands me and I check my watch. 'Plenty of time for you to be back before St Saviour's closes its doors,' he assures me.

As soon as I reach the High Street the memories roll in like the tide, fuelled by childhood familiarity and the ever-present squawk of seagulls. Oh, I've missed this place. Shops have changed hands, but it's essentially the same. 'A quaint English seaside town', is how the brochure describes it. I drop the leaflet in the first dustbin I find.

Tourists amble along the pavements, window-gazing, chatting, ice-cream cones clutched between sausage fingers. Smiles, sunglasses, shorts and t-shirts; that's what summer is about here. And tea shops selling home-made scones and clotted cream. I worked at the Scarlet Geranium tearoom one summer. It's where I first met Billy, his parents owned the place.

Ahead of me, a young family hogs the pavement; mother and father each hold the tiny hand of one of their offspring. Two adults, two children, the typical family. For a moment, it's as if I'm looking at my own children, Sally and Peter. I wonder how long it will take these youngsters to lose the innocence that allows them to return my smile and wave. I soon find out: our shared moment is broken when the mother slaps down the boy's hand, mid-wave. She bends and whispers something to him and his face loses its joy and becomes a mask, just like hers. He no longer skips or jumps over the cracks in the pavement. Poor kid. I wonder if he'll ever be as free as I was at his age. Things are different now. I see it with my own grandchildren.

The little girl looks just like Sally at the same age, and a forgotten fragment of memory surfaces. Gordon and I were going through a difficult patch. I was alone with the children for months at a stretch in the impersonal suburbs of London. I'd gone downstairs to see Mrs Foster, one of the few friendly faces in my loneliness, and stayed longer than I realised. When I returned, the flat was silent, toys abandoned. I found the children curled in bed together in their pyjamas, curtains closed. 'We thought you'd gone away, like Daddy,' Sally told me and my heart broke.

I move on, past the three art galleries, side by side. Once, a famous artist came to our seaside town and sat out on the pavement with an easel. She painted the church where Harrisons have been hatched, matched and dispatched for over a century. She painted the café opposite where people sit in the sun at wobbly tables and eat cream teas, children sipping Coca Cola through bendy straws. She painted the best of our town and sold her pictures to the eager tourists.

My favourite was her picture of the graveyard. You could even read the names on the gravestones. I liked it because Mum's gravestone was right in the middle of the picture. I used to stand and stare at it for ages, until old Mr Jenkins, the gallery owner, asked me to leave. He told me other people couldn't see in if I stood there all afternoon.

Mum had died the summer I turned eight.

'You look so like her,' Dad always said. I understood the pain in his eyes and it hurt, so I took the scissors to my hair when I was supposed to be asleep and stuffed the evidence inside my old teddy bear, whose innards were falling out of a hole in his back. Dad cried when he saw me the next morning. 'Oh, Martha love, what did you go and do that for?' He stroked the sticking up hair on my head. 'You were such an angel with all that golden hair.'

'I wanted to look like me, not Mum.' In truth, I looked like a yellow gooseberry. He'd closed his eyes and sighed. I guess I did the right thing. Sometimes it was hard to tell with him. He never spoke much and it got worse after Mum died. He was like a clam, closed tight against the world, until the drink opened his lungs and he shouted so much they banned him from the pub.

I remember Mum was the big talker in the family. My own children call me the chatterbox. I guess I am like her. I just wish I'd known her for longer; I wish she'd been around when I needed her guidance and advice. If only… Well there's one thing I've learned the hard way: there's no point wishing for something, you've got to do something about it.

That's why I'm here.

Ahead, a chunky couple gaze into the latticed bow window of Sweetest Candies and I wonder if *Made With Love* is still printed on every paper bag. I watch as their noses press the glass, hands either side of dimpled cheeks to shield the glare of the sun. The glass is smeared from many hands and noses and steamy breath. I used to clean that glass every Saturday morning, as soon as Mr Williams opened the shop. It was my first job of the day.

Mr Williams doesn't own the place any more. He's long gone. I remember how he'd give me broken pieces of peanut brittle from the trays. He didn't know I broke them on purpose. Well, maybe he did, but he always smiled that smile, the corners of his eyes crinkling like the sun's rays.

Mrs Williams—the catty-witch-lady we used to call her, with her jet black hair and those two deep furrows between her over-plucked eyebrows—used to frown at me all the time. I thought it was because of the peanut brittle. Back then, my innocence was dangerous. I didn't understand. If Mum had been around, things might have been different.

Dad's sister, Aunt Liz, took me to Munro's to buy my very first bra, a trainer bra they called it back then. How restricting it was, but how grown-up I felt, so I wore it with pride. Mr Williams, he wanted to see the daisies I told him were embroidered on the front. So I pulled up my top and showed him, right there in the back room, and he touched the daisies, said he was counting them. That's when Mrs Williams walked in, hissing and spitting at Mr Williams like a cat. 'Martha Harrison get out of here this instant,' she'd yowled at me. I never worked at Sweetest Candies again.

I've been so lost in reminiscing that I haven't been paying attention to where I'm going. My feet know the way. Gordon, Billy, and I used to ride our bikes to the beach every day in the summer, to play with friends, to swim. Now I stand and gaze up at the lighthouse swathed in its pristine red and white stripes, like a Christmas candy cane. It's been renovated and well maintained and I even notice the anemometer positioned near the edge of the cliff, its four cups barely moving today.

I overhear a tour guide explaining to a group of children, 'The lighthouse is here to warn ships not to get too close to shore. Those rocks out there are called the Monster's Teeth because they can tear into a boat.'

I look past the lighthouse and the sheer drop to the rocks below and I remember the windy night Billy Wadsworth's dad didn't come back from his fishing trip. How Billy, Gordon and I had forced open the padlocked lighthouse door and climbed the 297 narrow steps, round and round, all the way up to the viewing platform. I'd brought Dad's special binoculars, the ones with *Property of the Coastguard* engraved on the side. He'd told me the light could be seen for forty nautical miles. With strong binoculars, I figured we'd be able to see much farther than that. If Billy's dad's boat was out there, we'd be able to see its lights.

'Each lighthouse along the coast has a different set of light flashes so ships know where they are,' the tour guide explains. 'Now, who wants to go up inside?' An enthusiastic chorus of 'Me! Me! Me!' erupts from the children.

'We can't go into the lantern room, where the big light is, but we can go to the lightkeeper's catwalk. See the platform with the railing going all the way round? That's where we're going. It's a long climb to the top. Ready?' The group moves off towards the base of the lighthouse.

I turn to the beach where families congregate on beach towels. The remnants of a day on the beach surround them in organised chaos—picnic hampers, lopsided chairs sinking in the sand, striped beach umbrellas casting long shadows in the afternoon sun, buckets and spades scattered. Children dance in and out of the shallows, shrieking with joy at being chased by the waves, others crouching by sandcastles partially devoured by the incoming tide. I hear the buzzing drone of dune buggies, like the distant sound of a swarm of bees, and wish for a moment they'd been around back when I was a kid. That would have been fun…

But I'm not here for fun. I'm here to pay my respects to the teenager who died the same night his father's boat went missing. Billy Wadsworth, who was snatched from that catwalk. Billy Wadsworth, whose body lay broken on the Monster's Teeth until the coastguard found him. Dad said he would have died instantly.

Billy was in the same spot as Dad had found Mum's body. She used to dive from the Monster's Teeth. She must have hit her head and been washed back up onto the rocks…

I remember Billy climbing up on the railings and peering into the darkness with Dad's binoculars.

I remember the wind howling like a werewolf in a nightmare.

I remember screaming at Billy to come down, but he couldn't hear me.

I remember how Gordon and I wrapped our arms around Billy's skinny legs.

And I can never forget the haunting emptiness of my arms in that terrible moment… We had all been warned about the winds. We all knew why the lighthouse was off-limits.

Six men and one child died that night.

I feel the gentle sea breeze in my face and tears stream down my cheeks; I can taste their salty wetness. It's the wind making them water. It's not me, I'm all cried out: I cried for my Mum; I cried when Dad died a week before his first grandchild was born; I cried when my beloved Gordon succumbed to cancer last year. Oh how I miss him.

Yes, my love, I know we were meant to make this trip together… It's fifty years to the day.

Being here… at last I can cry tears for poor Billy. I never told a soul what happened, neither did Gordon. What cowards. We were the only ones who knew the truth and we carried the guilt. Everyone assumed Billy had been alone that night, searching the horizon for his father.

I glance at my watch. I'll have to hurry if I'm going to get back before they close St. Saviour's and the graveyard to visitors. It's time to find Billy's grave and to say the words I've held inside for so long. 'We should never have gone up there. We should have held you tighter. Billy… forgive us.'

The Ripped Veil

Jae Erwin

ELLA SHOOSHED THROUGH THE ANKLE-DEEP leaves covering the road down to her student flat. A half smile reached up from her toes as her faraway boyfriend snuck into her thoughts.

—*I love his long fingers.*

Sweet wood smoke from a suburban bonfire crept up her nose and the traffic burr faded enough for her to hear the chinking sound of a robin somewhere in the garden hedges. Solitary birdsong, bonfire smells and autumn damp: a perfect recipe for that old back-to-school lurch in her belly. Loneliness rubbed raw by coming to a new place, living amongst strangers.

—*Friday afternoon, no more lectures.*

Weekends held mixed blessings for her. The joy of lie-ins couldn't compete with the bleakness of the empty flat when the five girls she shared with left Belfast for their home towns and families. Ella wouldn't be seeing home again until Christmas; the flights to Manchester cost too much.

—*At least Robert will be phoning tonight.*

She checked the mail boxes and climbed the stairs to the top floor. A communal flat on either side of the stairs and a laundry room in the middle; each floor the same. The accommodations people kept girls, boys, Catholics and Protestants apart.

—*I wonder how they decided which flat to put me in?*

She was a girl of course, and a Catholic; but she was also English, which equated to being Protestant in many minds here. She was tolerated in both camps so long as she followed the unwritten rules— not too English, not too Catholic. She could walk that line, unattached to either idea. Even so, the watchfulness of her new flatmates itched between her shoulder blades.

Ella let herself in to the right-hand flat and padded past the other girls' doors, all closed, all silent, towards her room next to the kitchen.

—*Everybody must have gone.*

The short corridor was as quiet and dark as a church. A note taped to her door fluttered and her heart lifted: a message. 'Ring home before 4pm. Dad.'

—*Why is he ringing? I hope it's not too late.*

She scrunched her forehead as she glanced at her watch. Twenty to four.

She unlocked the door to her room, clunked her bag of books into the corner with her smelly trainers, rattled a handful of change from the phone-money tin and headed back out to the landing. The dripping washing in the laundry room added a meagre layer of sound-proofing for the phone on the wall. Each time she used the phone she squirmed at standing amongst other people's underwear like a pervert. So she turned her back to keep her eyes away from them; especially the boys' underpants.

'Hi Dad, I got your message.'

'We waited until the weekend to tell you.' Her father's voice, flat and low. 'Your Mum didn't want to interrupt your studies. It's bad news.'

The plunge of blood from Ella's face and stomach left her nauseous and breathless. She stiffened, ready. 'What is it?'

'Your Aunt Beth has been killed in a fall. They think she slipped on the canal path and hit her head. They say that she would have died almost instantly.'

Shock thumped into her gut. Ella staggered and banged into the wall. She clamped down on a low moan, clawing back control. 'When?'

'On Wednesday.'

The little crack of loneliness fractured apart into desolation. Tumbled images of a canal bank, of bright sunshine reflecting off the water and of a mossy shaded path replaced the washing lines and payphone.

—*Aunt Beth's favourite walk when she wanted to think.*

'Are you still there?' Her father, his voice as sharp as glass, sounded impatient.

'Yes.' She pulled in air with a huge effort, fighting against an invisible barrier.

'I didn't want to have to tell you like this. Your Mum's too upset to come to the phone. We're not here over the weekend, that's why I wanted to catch you before four.'

—*You're going away for the weekend? After this? You're leaving me...*

'I'll have to go Dad.' She barely squeezed the words past the howl held tight in her throat. 'I'll ring you later.' Force of habit, just words—her parents wouldn't be there anyway. Not waiting for a reply, she clattered the handset back onto its cradle. The world shrank to a narrow tunnel as she fell over her own feet, back to her room, tears pouring but still no sound from her stretched wide mouth.

—*Please let it be a mistake.*

Ella clicked her room door closed behind her.

'Oh God. Oh God. Ohhhhh Goooooooddd.' The low sounds pushed past the blockage. She collapsed into a heap on the floor like an abandoned ragdoll. 'Aaaunt Be…e…ethhhh.' Still trying to be quiet, trying to rock the pain away, but the thin walls gave no protection from curious flatmates—from Catherine in the next room.

A rap at her door. 'Ella? Are you okay?' Catherine's soft County Down accent muffled by the wood. She hadn't left yet.

—*Maybe her boyfriend's stuck in traffic.*

Ella half listened to her rational self, still processing despite the shock; talking to itself on automatic pilot. She pushed herself to her feet, struggling to make her trembling limbs work, and tugged at the door handle. She stared into her neighbour's eyes, trying to find something there that would make sense of the news.

—*I'm supposed to do or say something.*

Ella looked out from the centre of a whirlwind of confusion. The thoughts moved too fast for her to pluck one from the chaos.

Catherine intervened, giving Ella a clue where to start. 'What's the message about? Your Daddy didn't sound too good when I answered the phone earlier.'

'My aunt's dead.' Ella resisted the urge to open her mouth wide, to loosen the skin stretched tight across her face, around her skull: it wouldn't look good.

'Oh no! What happened?' Catherine's avid eyes opened wide.

'She slipped and hit her head.'

The doorbell rang.

Catherine twitched her head round like a terrier spotting prey. 'That'll be Donal. I have to go. Are you going to be all right?'

Ella nodded, a little stunned; she had no other option. Somewhere at the back of her mind she realised the question was a social nicety, not an offer of support. They barely knew each other. Ella was an outsider—and English.

'Well then, bye.' Catherine's breath caught on the goodbye.

Ella closed the door.

—Aunt Beth was still alive three days ago.

She tried to grasp at those three days like a life raft. Somehow, not knowing meant it hadn't happened, creating a little loop where time folded back on itself.

She sat on the edge of her bed, her arms folded, her tucked-in hands clasped hard to her ribcage as she rocked, her thoughts mired in confusion.

—She's too young to die.

Ella covered her eyes with her hands even though there was only herself to hide her grief from. A barrage of images poured into the darkness.

* * * *

Her Last Birthday Present.

Ella and Aunt Beth stood underneath the wrought iron arches of Manchester's Victoria train station.

'Here, it's early I know, but I couldn't wait.' Aunt Beth hopped from foot to foot.

Ella took the long, leather box and creaked open the lid. A slim gold watch glittered from its red satin nest.

'Happy twenty-first!'

Ella squeezed her hands and smile tight in surprise, her eyebrows and shoulders raised in unison. She closed the lid and flung her arms around Aunt Beth's neck.

Aunt Beth's New Baby.

They climbed the shaded back alley side by side—hands touching on the handle of the big old fashioned pram nestling Ella's new cousin, Matty.

'We could try those new Bird's Eye frozen pancakes for tea. What do you think?' her aunt asked, panting slightly from the steep hill.

Ella smiled. The warmth of being asked wrapped around her like a blanket.

The Get-Well-Soon Treat.

Aunt Beth's silhouette showed against the light falling into her spare bedroom. 'I brought you a slice of melon, your favourite.'

'Will you read Raggedy Anne again, please?' Aunt Beth's affection was so like basking in the grass in the sun, nose close to a ladybird, that Ella eked out every extra second.

'Yes, but it's straight to sleep afterwards, okay? You're not long out of hospital and sleep helps stitches to heal.'

The Stylish New Suit.

Delight ran rivulets down Ella's spine at the little skirt-and-waistcoat suit Aunt Beth had bought her.

Zig-zags—like in all the catalogues. 'For me?'

'Well, try it on. Let's see if it fits.'

Ella chewed her bottom lip as she wiggled the hook into the eye to fasten the waistcoat by herself. Tucking her head a little into her left shoulder, feeling the shy-heat creep into her face, she twirled in front of the mirror.

The First Date.

'He's asked me to the football club disco.' Ella, head down, cleaned the perming rollers in the backwash basin. The Saturday job at Aunt Beth's salon earned her extra spending money. Ella's nose ran from the ammonia and she shuddered at the hairs clinging to fingers but her cheeks glowed red with the excitement.

—*A real boy likes me!*

'Oooo. Do you want me to do your hair for you? Your make up?' Aunt Beth's eyes sparkled at the challenge. 'What are you going to wear?'

* * * *

A loud knock rattled her door. Ella jumped and the memories blinked out.

'Phone.' One of the boys from the flat across. She reached for a name—Tony, maybe? Catherine must have left the door to their flat on the snib.

'Okay.' More a croak than a word.

Darkness swamped the room.

—*How long have I been sitting here?*

She eased the stiffness out of her legs, crossed the room and fumbled for the light switch.

—*What time is it?*

Ella glanced at her watch.

—*She gave it to me.*

Six o'clock. Phone.

—*That'll be Robert.*

She forced herself into motion, followed the retreating silhouette through the front door and towards the laundry room. The phone receiver balanced on the phonebook shelf; Ella tensed her shoulders, bracing herself to pick it up before fear washed her away.

'Hi.' She managed the single sound but didn't know what to say next.

'How're you doin' doll?'

Only a squeak made its way through her closed throat as she hunched over the phone on the wall.

'Hello? Are you there?'

She swallowed hard to bring her voice under control. 'Yes. Aunt Beth's dead.' What else was there to say?

'You're joking me! How, when?'

'Wednesday... she fell and hit her head...' Each word a sob she pushed out between gritted teeth. 'She died outright... she wouldn't have known anything about it.'

—*Is that right? Is that what Dad said?*

'Oh doll, are you all right? Oh God, that's not right.' His distress trickled through the cotton wool in her mind. 'How old is...was she?'

—*Was. Oh God!*

The pain lashed through the numbness, she flinched as if she'd been whipped. 'Forty three.'

'Even younger than my Dad when he died. And the wee boy...oh God, poor Matty.'

The painful conversation didn't last long. There was little he could say, even less he could do, from the other side of the Irish Sea.

* * * *

Ella watched the numbers on her clock change: 11:05pm. She sat on the bed with her nightdress stretched over her chin-tucked knees, her breath coming faster at the thought of the dark.

—*Now!*

She scooted across the bed, over to the far wall, flicked the light off, leapt across the room, dived back into bed and yanked the duvet over her head. Fear clenched her body and mind, panted from her lungs—a small girl again, afraid of cybermen and crocodiles under the bed. Minutes passed as she silenced her breathing, strained to hear sounds of movement. The weight of spirits, of malevolent beings, pressed down on the covers, suffocating her.

—*I can't breathe.*

—*They'll get me if I put my head out.*

—*I can't breathe.*

Ella drowned in a terror she had no control over. She ripped the quilt away and threw herself back through the darkness to the wall, scrabbling to find the switch before something grabbed her hand.

—*Where is it? Where is it?*

Panic shredded rational thought until her fingers touched smooth wood.

—*To the left; it's to the left of the door.*

She let out her breath, only aware she'd been holding it as the light flooded every corner. She stared at the curtain around her clothes rail, watching for movement in the green fabric, for the creeping fingers of fear to coalesce into something visible.

The rational part of her mind tried to intervene.

—*For God's sake, I'm a grown woman, it's a curtain.*

—*But I can feel it. The room's full of dead things. Is one of them her?*

—*No. She wouldn't hurt me.*

—*Who are they then?*

—*Go back to bed. Leave the light on. Say some Hail Marys. That always used to work.*

—*I gave that up long ago.*

—*Just do it!*

She ran across the room and vaulted the last couple of feet, unable to squash the fear of something grabbing her ankles. Back in bed, she pulled the duvet tight around her neck and pressed her spine against the wall. From there she watched the room, eyes forced wide, waiting. Her heartbeat thumped, du-dum, against damp skin in the hollow at her collar bones; her throat was scratchy from stifled sobbing.

'Hail Mary, full of grace, the Lord is with thee. Blessed art thou amongst women…'

Over and over again she whispered, seeking protection of The Mother. The words ran into one another, creating a protective barrier against the dead ones. Ella fought against the weight of her eyelids, trying to focus on the room and pull away from the shadowlands on the edge of sleep. Her head softened onto her pillow…

She jerked awake, checking nothing had crept up on her whilst her eyes were closed.

Eventually, exhaustion won out and she slept.

She woke time and again into a carnival of hallucinations—bright, constantly shifting, larger than life—unable to distinguish between reality, nightmare and fever-madness. Colours flashed, voices approached and retreated, presences pressed at her shoulder. Ella writhed in sweat-soaked sheets, shivering. Her sore throat had turned to ground glass, rasping red flesh raw each time she swallowed.

A hand shook her awake. No-one stood beside her even though she'd caught a glimpse of grey movement seconds earlier.

—*I'm dreaming.*

She awoke from being awakened; nobody there.

And again, certain that this time the dream would end.

And again, like the reflection of a mirror in a mirror, in a mirror.

—*Am I awake or dreaming?*

Aunt Beth beckoned. Ella pumped every ounce of effort into her legs and arms, running to reach her aunt, to hold her. She ran but stayed fixed to the spot.

—*What am I doing wrong?*

The harder she ran, the more she stayed put. Frustration brought her fists either side of her ears, and her roar blasted past clenched teeth.

Dream blackness engulfed her.

A gargoyle face punched a hole through, hurtling to within a hair's breadth of her nose; protruding eyes and lolling tongue.

Slam. A wall of pure rage hit her, knocked her dream-body backwards. Ella screamed herself awake for real this time.

* * * *

Time played tricks on her, rushing forward then slowing down. The last glance at the clock showed a leap of five hours, taking her into the afternoon. Ella dragged herself into the kitchen next door. Her hands did things, filled the kettle, took out a mug and a milk carton, of their own volition. She watched from a place outside of herself, disinterested, only going through the motions. Two competing forces pressed in on her. One stretched itself thin and taut as a drum head and held something back, something dangerous. The other, sharp, worked in direct opposition, trying to pierce, to rend.

Someone banged on the door to the flat. Ella weaved and staggered down the hallway, bracing her hand along the wall for support. Arms trembled, weak, powerless as she scrabbled at the lock and pulled the door open.

'Ella!'

She stood, mute.

—*Robert?*

Her thoughts stuck there, unable to take the next step.

'Ella?' He caught hold of her arm as she wobbled. 'You look awful.'

He stepped through and pushed the door closed with his foot as he moved one arm around her waist and hoisted his bag in the other hand. 'I got a last minute flight from Manchester. I couldn't let you be on your own. I have to go back early on Monday for work though.' He glanced at the doors on either side. 'Which one's your room? They all look the same.'

Ella pointed back down towards the kitchen, her arm almost too heavy to lift. Their shoulders and hips bumped, throwing each other out of step, causing them to stagger the short distance to her bedroom door. Robert pushed the door wide with his sports bag, threw it on the floor and pulled her into the circle of his arms. Her body complied, arms limp at her sides. The pressure of holding in the sobs trying to force their way out burned through her lungs.

'It's okay to cry you know,' he mumbled into the hood of her dressing gown. 'Here, sit down and I'll make us a cup of tea.'

She listened to him clattering around the kitchen, opening cupboards, probably trying to find things. The smell of toast filtered through, making her stomach rumble.

—*He's flown all the way over here.*

A feeling of unease stirred deep in her belly.

—*Why's he done that?*

Robert barged the door open with his backside, balancing plates of toast on top of the mugs of tea. 'I don't suppose you've eaten today either have you?'

Ella shook her head.

—*I'm not hungry.*

She wiped the thin sheen of sweat from her face with her dressing gown sleeve.

Using his forearm he eased aside books, pens and colour-coded files of research. The metal parts screeched across the surface of the desk and the books closest to the edge thudded onto the floor as he put the mugs down on the desk.

'Uh, sorry.' Robert bent to pick the books up, straightened and opened his mouth as if to speak, closed it again. He took a breath. 'I don't know what to do. What can I do to help?'

'Can you get them to leave my bedroom?' Ella whispered, afraid they would hear her and take revenge.

Robert scanned the room, his eyebrows pulled together. 'Them? What do you mean, Ella?'

She bent forward, shoulders hunched around her ears creating a secret space. 'The sharp thing and the stretched thing.'

Robert's eyes widened.

'See, that's what I mean. You feel them too, don't you?'

'Ella, there's nothing here in the room. Just you and me.'

She drew back from him and lifted her chin. 'So whose side are you on then? The sharp or the stretched? Which one are you working for?' Eyes squeezed narrow, her voice rose. 'Tell me now. If it's the sharp thing I want you to leave right now.'

Robert rocked back from the blast of anger, then stepped forward, his arms reaching. Ella shifted back, so he dropped his arms to his sides, rubbing his palms on the sides of his jeans. 'I'm working for you,

Ella. Here, drink your tea.' His voice quavered as he passed the mug to her. 'Now, tell me about the sharp thing and the…'

'…the stretched thing,' Ella finished for him, nodding now that he seemed to understand how important it was, leaning forward a little. 'The stretched thing, it's holding things back, bad things. It's stopping them from coming through. The sharp thing's pointed. It's trying to tear the stretched thing—to let the bad things in.'

'Can I just check something?' Robert asked, inching forward to the edge of the bed where he sat. 'I'll have to touch you.'

Ella nodded.

He moved closer and put his hand to her forehead. 'You're really hot. Do you think, maybe, this is…the things you can feel…maybe it's a fever and the shock? I mean…'

'What are you trying to say? That they're not real? I can feel them. Are you saying I'm mad?'

'No, no!' He rubbed his hands along his thighs.

Ella watched him closely for signs of deceit.

—*Is he a sharp thing?*

Robert seemed to be thinking, his eyes up towards the ceiling. 'What if we could support the stretched thing—do you think that would help? I read somewhere about using visualization in healing. You use pictures to help. I don't really know how, but maybe it would work.'

Ella took a deep breath.

—*Yes.*

'The stretched thing—oh—it's Aunt Beth. It's her trying to seal the rip. She likes that idea.' Ella beamed a smile at Robert.

He shifted his shoulders and smiled back but didn't meet her eyes. 'Maybe you need to see a doctor too…' Ella started to interrupt but he pushed on, forcing her to listen. 'Just to help you with the shock. I don't really know what I'm doing. I'll help you with the stretched thing…'

'Aunt Beth!'

'…Aunt Beth, but we need others to help keep the sharp thing out too.'

'I don't need a doctor.'

'Please, just for me.' Robert looked right into her eyes.

'Doctors can't keep the sharp thing out! They can't even see it.' Ella huffed out her breath.

'But they can help with the fever. You're too hot, that's dangerous too. I need to be sure we've covered everything.' Robert had his hands on her knees now. 'It'll make me feel better.'

Ella tilted her head to one side, listening to Aunt Beth. 'Okay, I'll go to the doctor…'

Robert's shoulders softened and he blew out a breath.

'…but we need to work on this now.'

He nodded. 'How do you want to do it?'

'Spiders.'

'Spiders?' Robert shuddered and Ella fired a hysterical bullet of laughter.

—He's scared of spiders.

'They make strong webs. We can use spiders to repair the hole. Aunt Beth's stretched too thin, trying to close the rip in the veil.'

* * * *

Ella coached herself as she made her way from the baggage-collection area. 'Don't cry…Don't cry…Don't cry,' under her breath. A man in a grey suit stared at her. Ella tightened her lips together.

—Enough people think I'm mad as it is.

She shuffled into the arrivals area of Manchester airport and strained onto her tiptoes, trying to see around the lumpy shoulders of the couple in front of her.

—There he is! Matty.

Her little cousin; his blond head shone like a beacon.

Robert and Uncle Richard flanked him. Robert had gone home ahead of her once they'd seen the doctor and the medications started to calm her.

'Ella!' Matty's high-pitched voice pierced the airport rumble.

Uncle Richard spotted her and waved, his face grey and unmoving.

—Don't cry, you'll upset them.

—Spider's web.

The veil strengthened.

She fixed on her smile and held in the tears as she hugged Matty and Uncle Richard.

'The car's this way,' said Uncle Richard. He put his arm around his son's shoulders and steered him through the clusters of people. Robert and Ella followed.

Robert slipped his hand into hers. 'How're you doing?' he asked quietly. 'Are you still taking the tablets?'

'Yes.'

'What did the student counsellor say?'

'She called it a temporary psychosis brought on by shock, stress.'

'What about the—'

'—the rip's still there. Aunt Beth's still holding it together, but it's getting smaller.'

'Right.' He squeezed her fingers. She heard the doubt.

'The counsellor, Gillian, she said the rip isn't real, nor the gargoyle, none of it. Aunt Beth isn't really there. They're all aspects of me; of my personality.' Ella watched the worry lines soften on Robert's face as her words had the desired effect.

* * * *

Two days later Ella and Matty climbed out of the car and stood on the pavement outside the Wimpy burger bar in the city centre. Her cousin clung to her hand as if it were his first day at school.

'I'll look after him, Uncle Richard. If there's a problem and he needs to come back to you, I'll ring straight away. I've got all the telephone numbers here.' Ella pulled the piece of paper from her coat pocket. 'Don't worry.'

Uncle Richard nodded. 'Thanks, love.'

She'd offered to take Matty to the cinema while Uncle Richard finalized funeral and legal matters. Matty stepped forward, dragging Ella with him, and slammed the car door shut. Uncle Richard crunched the gears, turned to give them a sheepish grin and shoulder shrug and, with a blast of diesel fumes, pulled out into the city traffic.

A flutter of panic rippled through Ella.

—What now? How do I let him know I'm here for him?

'Do you want to get something to eat before we go?' she asked, nodding at the burger place.

'No, I'm not hungry.' Matty looked anywhere but in her eyes, his face a bleak wasteland.

—He's trying not to cry.

'We can get ice cream or popcorn in there if you want, or something after the film.'

He nodded and tightened his grip.

* * * *

The adverts had started by the time they eased into their places. Empty seats surrounded them. Ella hadn't thought to check the films beforehand so they had to resort to Electric Dreams, the only one twelve-year-old Matty could get into. The film trundled on in front of her unseeing eyes as she watched the spiders swinging on gossamer, weaving the spiral threads. With each new web the tear in the veil shrank.

Aunt Beth whispered.

—Almost safe.

'Do you think she's watching us?' the little boy murmured into the dark.

Ella hesitated.

—Will it scare him? Aunt Beth, what do I tell him?

A hum rose through the threads.

She turned to him. 'She'll be here for you as long as you need her.'

Matty looked straight ahead but she saw his profile moving in the lights of the film as he nodded. 'That's what I thought too. I feel her close by sometimes—when I'm missing her really badly.'

Ella stroked his cheek.

* * * *

Something was amiss. Ella sat in the pub around the corner from the home she and Robert bought after they got married. Her velvet-cushioned stool stood way too tall for the table, leaving her stranded in mid-air. She couldn't reach the table with her elbows and her feet dangled, making her back ache.

—That's not right. The stools aren't like that.

The browns of the décor smouldered in the light from the small windows but the angles looked wrong; everything was too far away. Ella felt the wrongness as a tug on her solar plexus, pulling her to resolve it.

Uncle Richard and Matty were in the dining room next door. She glanced again at the stone archway...

—It should be a door.

...shoulders tight, afraid they'd come through.

Aunt Beth sat beside her, ethereal, not quite there. 'I've got to go now but I don't want to upset them.' She nodded towards the other room.

'Do you have to go?' Ella asked. The warm familiarity of Aunt Beth comforted her.

'Yes, but I couldn't go without letting you know, without saying goodbye.' A soft wave wrapped itself around Ella and then whisked away like a silk scarf caught in the wind.

She woke with a sob and rolled to her side, staring at the orange street light reflecting off the louvered wardrobe doors, through the gap in the bedroom curtains.

—*Aunt Beth came to me.*

The weight of losing her again pressed down on Ella, pinning her to the bed. The desolation tore at her as strong as two years earlier, despite the counselling.

—*Spiders? Are you there?*

Silence. The rip in the veil sealed.

—*She's finally gone.*

Ella tried to muffle the moan in her pillow.

'What's the matter?' Robert spoke out of the dark.

'Aunt Beth visited me. She came to say goodbye.'

'What?'

'In my dream. It was so real, she was so real.'

'It was just a dream.'

'No. It felt real. She sat beside me. She said she had to go now.' Ella's tears streaked her face and dampened her pillow. 'The spiders have gone too.'

'That's a good thing isn't it?' She heard the higher note of fear in his voice. 'It means you don't need them anymore. They were just an idea to help you through a tough time. That's what your counsellor said.'

'…Yes.'

—*It's what he needs to hear.*

Robert rolled over and curled around her body, his forearm over hers, their fingers knit together.

Ella breathed out and closed her eyes.

* * * *

Ella fidgeted beside Robert at the end of the top table in the beautifully decorated community hall. Fresh flowers and ribbons garlanded doors and tables. Harriet, Matty's bride, owned a florist's shop and had done it all herself.

—I can't believe it's twelve years since our wedding.

She pulled her wedding ring over her knuckle and rotated it round and round her finger.

'I'd like to thank you all for coming and making this a special day for Matty and Harriet…' Ella tuned out of Uncle Richard's speech.

—Aunt Beth would have loved all this, the hairdos, the make-up, the dresses and masses of flowers.

The hall shimmered with Harriet's wedding gown, manicured women in beautiful cocktail dresses, men in morning suits, and shining silverware.

'…There is of course one person who isn't here today: Matty's mum, Beth.' Gruff Uncle Richard, who had battled his way through fourteen years of being a widower, stopped and breathed hard. Ella froze in the face of his unravelling emotions.

'She would have been in her element here…' His voice ran up a scale like a pianist and broke at the top. Ella glanced at Matty; he had a handkerchief covering his eyes.

—Shit!

The wedding speeches ignited hot grief in Ella, a searing pain, and panic flared in her chest. She gripped the edge of the table, the ground tilting beneath her, and turned to Robert, her face rigid with fear. Her husband's expression slipped from the soft smile of sympathy to the hard mask of recognition. He twisted in his seat, clasped her hand tight.

'Grip my fingers—you remember the routine. Put both your feet on the ground and weave the spiders' webs. Fight it; keep it out.' He kept his voice low. 'I'm right here beside you. Can you last through the speeches?'

Ella couldn't pull the meaning from his words. Images and gut-rocking sensations from fourteen years ago swooped up out of the tangle of pain.

—Spiders' webs; strong, elastic.

Ella heard the reassuring whisper of their spinning. She opened her eyes to Robert's; his hands holding her firm.

I can do this.

SCORCHED EARTH

CATH MURPHY

T HE THIRD AND LAST TIME it happened was at the Thornes' barbecue. Connie hadn't been there either of the other times, but she had heard about them.

The first time was in Waitrose. Delighted whispers in the car park. *Yes, in Waitrose... Marjorie Thorne! ... Opened a water bottle and poured it all over herself.* People were bound to gossip really. The Thornes had the house, the horses, the smart new cars. Everyone wanted to know them, but everyone also rather enjoyed the idea that they might be less than perfect.

Connie just missed seeing the second incident. She was in the shower towelling off after a game of badminton when a shout came from the swimming pool. By the time Connie was dressed, it was all over. Marjorie had been plucked from the pool by the lifeguard and was already being driven home by one of the cafeteria staff. *Fully dressed... in the middle of Aquarobics...She's having a breakdown!*

But that was three weeks ago and since then Marjorie had been her usual, rather quiet self. Connie saw her in the florists the day before the barbecue, arms full of bright red roses—at least a hundred pounds' worth, but that was the Thornes for you, no expense spared. Connie confirmed that she and Tom would be coming. You would have thought Marjorie would have been grateful for the support, after what had happened, but she just blinked and smiled faintly and walked off to her huge shiny Range Rover, the flower heads bobbing submissively as she went.

Perhaps it had been a minor breakdown. Connie sipped her champagne—Tom had told Peter you could get a pretty decent Cava for around a tenth of the price, but Peter just said he had the money, he might as well spend it—and watched Marjorie set out bowls of salad. While the wives clustered in groups, exchanging small talk and compliments, the men stood by the barbecue, some great shiny gas arrangement, watching Peter prodding at the steaks. Men could never just let food cook. They always had to be fiddling with it, as if it had to pay better attention.

Conversation drifted over. Peter was holding forth, as was his right, Connie supposed. He was the host. She half-listened, swirling the strawberry round and round in her glass.

They called it scorched earth... on the television last night... really quite interesting...

Marjorie went into the house and came out again with a basket of rolls. Connie had offered to help, but Marjorie had refused, a little sharply, as if she felt Connie were interfering. But then, Connie thought charitably, Marjorie was probably tired of over-solicitous friends.

Scorched earth. Connie took another sip of her drink. The phrase had a familiar sound, but she couldn't place it. Something to do with the weather? The heat wave was into its second week, with no sign of letting up. The hosepipe ban had turned the lawns to yellow and frazzled rectangles. Connie let her gaze wander over the fields beyond the Thornes' large and rather smart garden—they had a man in twice a week to keep it tidy—until it rested on the far trees, some rather nice elms which had escaped viral ravages, but whose branches were now weighted by a flock of large and sullen looking crows.

Tom had noticed the crows too. *Dear Tom.* Connie felt a rush of affection for her husband, who was patient about the Thornes even though Peter could be so overbearing about his business successes, name-dropping and peppering his anecdotes with implausibly large sums of money. Tom was pointing to the birds, asking a question.

Had to get a shotgun to scare them off in the end... Slim pickings for them with this drought...

Peter doused the steaks with something from a bottle and the flames roared up briefly, much to the delight of the crowd. Marjorie left entertaining the guests to her husband, but that was often how it worked with couples—one doing nice, while the other dealt with the practical side of things. Although, right now, Marjorie wasn't doing either. She had set down the basket of bread and wandered away from the table to look at the feature in the middle of the dried-up lawn. As Connie focused on her, Marjorie started to walk slowly over the dead grass, like a sleepwalker.

If Connie had given any conscious thought to what the Thornes had in the middle of their garden, she might have moved more quickly. But the pond was so heavily coated in duck weed, it looked deceptively solid. By the time Connie realised what was going to happen, Marjorie was already calf-deep in water.

'Marjorie!' Connie started to run. At the edge of the pond she stretched out a hand, but couldn't reach. Marjorie appeared not to hear her. Mushroom clouds of slime billowed to each side as she sat down.

'Not this again.' Peter arrived at Connie's side, a pair of tongs in his hand. 'Get out, right now!'

Marjorie lay back in the water and draped a handful of weed over her face. She seemed rather serene, as if she were quite alone and not surrounded by a group of astonished friends and neighbours.

'I've had enough of this!' Peter was red-faced, shouting. 'Someone get her out!'

'Poor dear, it must be this heat,' said one of the women comfortably.

Thank goodness for dear, practical Tom. There he was, rolling up his trouser legs, stepping into the pond. 'Nip into the house and fetch a towel, would you?' he asked Connie. It was just the kind of sensible suggestion he would make; so much more helpful than Peter's anger.

Inside it smelled musty, an empty-house scent of damp, and it was dark, all the curtains drawn against the heat, Connie supposed, although in this weather you'd want all the windows open, not covered up with those heavy velvet drapes. The curtains were very Peterish: he went in for all that Baronial stuff. Suits of armour and tapestries on the wall. Which was fine if you had a house the right size and could afford it.

Connie pressed a light switch, but nothing happened. The bulb must have blown. She felt her way down a corridor—wasn't the downstairs loo somewhere along here?—and emerged in what she assumed must be Peter's study, judging by the massive kneehole desk, dark and highly polished. She flicked the light switch but, again, nothing happened.

God it was hot in here. The grate was full of ashes and the bitter tang of smoke hung in the air—he'd had a fire going, in this weather!

She really had to open a window. Connie dragged back the curtains, the heavy folds brushing her face in a most unpleasant, almost vital way, and tugged at the bottom of the sash. It refused to budge, even by a fraction. The heat must have swollen the wood. She put a wrist to her forehead and turned back into the room. Now the curtains were drawn, she could see better.

Peter had been burning paper in the fire—sheaves of it. How peculiar. A half-open cupboard by the desk revealed more paper, a jumble of letters and envelopes layered to a depth that was almost geological.

Connie jumped at the sound of raised voices from outside. She hastily retreated into the corridor, searching for the loo and a towel, and nearly fell over an object propped up against the wall. A shotgun. *The crows...* Crazy to leave a shotgun lying around like that!

There was a transmission whine coming from one of the rooms further along the corridor. Connie peeked in: a huge plasma television was playing nothing but static. In here, too, it was stifling, but the window was stuck. All the windows were stuck.

Connie couldn't say why she picked up the phone, or why she wasn't surprised when she heard the hollow hiss of the empty line.

The house was dead. Nothing moved, nothing breathed. Connie fled to the kitchen—high-tech, equipped to within an inch of its life—snatched a tea towel from the back of a chair, and ran out the back door.

She was too late. Peter was marching Marjorie—dripping and muddy, trailing the smell of pond weed—in through the front of the house. He slammed the door in the faces of his startled guests. Connie caught a final glimpse of Marjorie's face, a pale moon in the shadow.

'*Quite* a turn up for the books.' Tom's trousers were dark from the knee down and a muddy handprint decorated the front of his polo shirt. 'She needs help, if you ask me.'

The house disappeared in the rearview mirror. The clammy panic which had gripped Connie receded with it, but she knew that if she went back, it would be waiting for her, in the patient corners of the panelling, the expensive, unnecessary gadgets in the kitchen, the costly and garish upholstery of the giant three piece suite in Peter's vast living room. She thought again of Marjorie's dumb white face in the shadow of the hall, almost pleading...

'Why does he buy all that stuff? The cars, the furniture. Marjorie doesn't want it. I don't even think Peter wants it, except to show it to other people.' Connie knew she sounded petty, meanly jealous, but she couldn't help saying it.

Tom shrugged, steering with one hand, elbow on the sill. 'No idea. Pride maybe. Peter's the type who hates to lose at anything. Golf, squash, even a game of pool at the pub. Dislikes losing face.'

Scorched earth. That phrase came to her again. The faint smell of smoke was still hanging around. It must be in her hair. She'd have a nice long shower when she got home. Connie thought of water and shivered. Poor Marjorie. Connie pictured her in the aisle at Waitrose, the bottle upended over her head, her hair darkening into damp tendrils, the puddle growing around her feet.

'What were you talking about while Peter was cooking?'

Tom turned to her, mildly puzzled at the sharpness of her tone. 'I don't remember particularly. Peter was banging on about some big contract he'd just landed. Sounded slightly made up, but then that's par for the course with him. Always tell myself to divide by two where he's concerned.'

'That's not what I mean. He said something about scorched earth. What was that about?'

'Oh that! Some programme he'd been watching on the telly. History thing, a tactic the Germans used in the Second World War. A bit extreme, but then the Germans were extreme.'

The Thornes' house was well behind them now, hidden behind those big elms which fringed the field. The crows were still roosting there, like strange, moody fruit. But as Connie craned around for a better look, the birds lifted all at once, like so many flakes of ash in the wind.

'I remember now,' Tom continued, voice easy. *Dear Tom.* The words snagged frantically in Connie's brain as her eyes scanned the view out of the back window. 'When the Germans were in retreat, they burned the land behind them and everything in it so the enemy couldn't use it against them. They scorched the earth...'

Dear Tom. Look behind... Oh dear God, Tom.

'Can you smell smoke?' he asked, sniffing the air.

THE STAR GAZER TRIBUNE

WILLIAM D. WEBB, JR.

A SHAGGY HAIRED COLLEGE STUDENT perused an advertisement for filters. Not your ordinary filters, like oil or air, but something different.

'This is very odd,' he said, pushing blond hair out of his eyes.

The ad appeared in a tabloid known only to science fiction buffs, nerds and extra-terrestrial fanatics: The Star Gazer Tribune, circulation 150, as noted on the front page. It read:

> *Scintar Farmers Seeking Filters*
>
> *Do you always know the right answer, never lose at cards, always win in Vegas? Can you tell when someone is lying, deceitful, or just plain rude?*
>
> *Maybe you're a Fact Filter?*
>
> *Are your friends and family totally annoyed with your honesty?*
>
> *Do you always hit the nail on the head?*
>
> *Maybe you're a Truth Sayer?*
>
> *If so, come see us. We'd love to talk with you. We are the Scintar Farming Cooperative, a for-profit regime that detests having machines do our thinking. In fact, it's illegal on our planet.*
>
> *If selected, you may be eligible for ridiculous pay and even more ridiculous benefits. Applications are being taken this Saturday at:*
>
> *University of California, Berkley.*
>
> **Try not to get killed!**

Pictures of sunny beaches and mounds of cash surrounded the ad.

'Try not to get killed?' the student said, scanning the page. He rolled up the paper, flipping it under his arm, and pushed his hands in the pockets of his brown leather trench coat. His was a standard college uniform that told everyone that he didn't conform. He scowled at the horizon. A darkened midday sky loomed over the university, but it wasn't from clouds or a storm.

'Awful lot of them, doncha think, Mr. Stash, my man?' he said to his companion.

'Farmers?' said Stash. He was a taller boy, stocky, with a long thin nose He had a matching coat and long blond hair. 'More like an invasion, Mr. Quay. The Tribune says they're here to farm Earth.' He brandished his copy of the Tribune. 'See,' he said tapping the front page.

'I see,' said Quay, wiping his nose on a sleeve.

Above them, swarming like locusts, flew a fleet of aircraft too bulky to be jet planes, more like floating battleships. There were massive helicopters, too, and some hovering dark rectangles resembling huge buildings, defying gravity. People on the ground, students and faculty, either wandered aimlessly or raced from building to building, pointing and screaming.

The two disheveled students strolled along the sidewalk less concerned with the howling humans that ran past them than with the overhead spectacle.

Quay snatched the Tribune and flipped to the back page. 'It says they farm fact filters and truth sayers,' he said. 'My stepdad farms cattle.'

'I hear it's a good gig. Lots of perks,' said Stash.

'Awfully loud, though, for aliens,' said Quay, arching his neck toward the sky. 'Shouldn't they have, like, anti-gravity or something?'

'Yeah,' said Stash, 'they have anti-gravity the way a jumbo jet with engine trouble has anti-gravity. Look, one of them is landing near the Student Union.'

Stash grimaced as a grinding explosion shook the earth. A blue, saucer-shaped craft as big as a football stadium crashed to the ground.

'Correction,' grunted Stash, '*on* the Union.'

Several large panels fell from the ship's sides. Two-legged creatures in bright blue riot gear poured out of the ship, some holding cattle prods while others wielded heavy firearms.

'They're heading this way,' said Quay.

'Perhaps they are hungry,' suggested Stash.

'Take me to your burger,' said Quay, smiling.

'You know they eat anything that has meat on it,' said Stash. He winced as a woman in pink sweats hurried past screaming.

'They eat people? Where did you hear that?' asked Quay, scowling at the screaming throng. 'I'd offer up my stepdad.'

Stash brandished the paper. 'There's a pull-out section on the whole invasion in this morning's edition, right next to the Walmart ad.'

The armada filled the sky and the sun appeared to set in the mid-afternoon. Blue-clad creatures fanned out in tight groups of four carrying assault weaponry. These appeared to be the soldiers. Behind them marched tall, thin, iguana-type figures in straw hats—the farmers?—wielding shiny metal prods and nasty long cylinders. Hovering above them, huge, heavily armed helicopters provided air support. Acrid smoke filled the air, and the screams of the fleeing crowds filled the space not already occupied by smoke.

'Do you suppose we are fact filters?' asked Stash.

'Maybe truth sayers?' said Quay.

'Or both. It says right here on the front page that most subscribers have some talent—all 150 of us.'

'I don't know. I bombed my theoretical physics final,' said Quay, scratching his head.

'You never did like the theoretical.'

Quay stepped sideways, avoiding two young men in full sprint. 'Watch it,' he said to them. 'You know I'm wondering whether it was a good idea to leave Tahoe.'

Stash arched his neck, scanning the sky. 'We've never really belonged here.'

An older man in a white uniform pointed up and screamed at them, 'Run you fools!'

'It's on the to-do list,' said Stash to the man's receding back.

'Yeah, but of all the aliens in the galaxy, why these Scintar dudes? I mean, I'm looking for beaches and babes, the easy life.'

'We'll get that,' said Stash

'Dude, they're lizards. What are we going to get? Lizard babes?'

The line of helicopters descended, stirring up dust and debris.

'Really loud, man, really loud!' shouted Stash as something came thundering over the rows of armed Scintar. It was a bulky craft nearly a mile wide and half as tall, with hundreds of jets firing at the ground to keep it aloft. It had vertical fins and was windowless and nearly featureless except for its close resemblance to a factory.

'What is that?' shouted Stash.

Quay serenely read a folded page. 'It looks to be a sorting machine.'

The craft slowly moved over the boys, whirling dust and bits of earth about their heads.

'What?' yelled Stash.

'It says here,' continued Quay, shouting, 'that sorting machines are used to harvest the talent, filters and such, and to, you know...' He stopped and squinted at the paper.

'And to what?'

Quay looked up at the incredible flying building, eyes ablaze.

'And to do what?' repeated Stash, snatching the paper from his friend. 'The lower floors house the filters, the uppers floors are a... a slaughterhouse?'

'They gotta eat.' Stash shrugged. 'You ready?'

Quay wiped dirt out of his eyes. 'I suppose they would have found us eventually anyway, but this sure is a weird way to take job applications.'

The earth rumbled and rolled under their feet, tossing them around like marbles in a blender. The sorting machine had landed.

'You don't suppose,' growled Quay, his face pinned against the sidewalk, 'that we might be chosen instead of eaten?'

Stash rolled onto his side and sat up, spitting dust and choking on smoke. 'If I were going to be chosen,' he said, removing grass from his lips, 'I wouldn't be this scared. Right? Being a fact filter and all I would know not to be, like, petrified.'

'Well I know and I'm not scared,' said Quay.

'The heck you aren't. I can tell, you know!'

'See, you are a fact filter,' said Stash, feigning a smile.

'Oh shut up.'

Quay rose on one knee. The air was even thicker with smoke and debris, tiny pieces of earth that would not be settling back any time soon.

One of the farmer-lizards approached them through the gray fog. Stash waved to it and it tipped its straw hat. 'Move along, kiddies, we have a schedule to keep.'

Quay whispered to Stash, 'Jesus Christ, they speak English.'

Stash shook his head. 'I don't think that's English.'

The farmer cocked its oval head at the boys, and a thin smile slid over even thinner lips. 'You understand me, both of you?'

Stash nodded.

'Come then,' said the farmer. 'You'll make my bonus for the period.'

Nearby, a mechanical crab the size of a dirigible was casually peeling the bricks off a dormitory. When it encountered the invariably screaming, flailing human behind the walls, it sucked the poor soul into a blue tube—gently, but without permission. One by one, the buildings crumbled.

Stash helped Quay to his feet. 'Like we have a choice?'

The farmer spoke into his blue lapel. 'I may have found something.' He looked back at the boys with cold, jet-black eyes. 'Choice? Always have a choice.'

Quay pointed at the thumping helicopters and frowned at the building-munching machine. 'Dying isn't much of a choice.'

Stash waved off his friend. 'So, tell us about the babes.' He pointed to two co-eds running in circles just to his left. 'Sort of like them, without the hysteria?'

The farmer nodded towards the sorting machine. 'Nope.'

Stash was not amused. 'I told ya we should have brought Val and Lisa with us.'

'Dude, even they think we're weird.'

'Yeah, but they don't have scales.'

Stash and Quay joined the thousands of other dirty, frightened humans being herded towards the smoking sorting machine.

'What's going to happen to all these people?' said Stash.

The farmer surveyed the crowd. 'They will be released back into the wild.'

'Really?'

'Or slaughtered,' it said. 'But between you and me, you're too salty to eat.'

Stash clutched his friend around the neck. 'Ever see that old Twilight Zone episode where the Martians convince all these people to visit their planet?'

'No,' said Quay, hanging on tightly to Stash's arm. 'Don't worry,' he called out to a group huddled nearby. 'We're all too salty.'

'Please keep moving,' said the farmer. 'Not far now.'

Stash continued, 'They disarm the planet and put these shields over all the cities, dismantle all their defense and weapon systems.' He stepped over an old man curled up into the fetal position and sucking his thumb. 'Then they give the earthlings a book.'

'You know what,' said Quay, slipping out of Stash's grasp and patting the farmer on the shoulder like an old friend. 'I'm not going in that machine.'

'Yes you are,' said the farmer. 'I said please.'

'The book is titled *To Serve Man.*' said Stash.

'So they, like, help, right?' said Quay.

'No no, it's a cookbook, to serve man, get it? It was definitely a Rod Sterling thing, great episode.'

'I'm out of here.' Quay waved to the farmer and turned away, but his head snapped back as an electric shock coursed though his arms. He slumped to the ground. Stash ran to him, fighting through several frightened exchange students.

'Did that hurt?' offered Stash. 'It looked like it hurt.'

'Sorry,' said the farmer. 'But you're worth a lifetime of barter.'

'Like don't we have our own army?' grumbled Quay. 'Where the hell is it?'

Stash slapped his forehead. 'I dunno. Did you notice the advance armada of alien lizards?'

The farmer said, 'I would suggest not doing that again.'

Before Stash or Quay could answer, the air above them seemed to explode.

'Now what?' growled Stash.

'Incoming fiberoids!' shouted the lizard, ducking. 'Time to go. NOW!'

'Fiber whats?' said Quay.

The lizard lunged at Quay, sending another jolt through his chest. 'Don't be coy with me. Where did you get them?'

Flying trees whizzed over their heads, scattering humans and aliens alike. The air instantly filled with anti-aircraft fire and the roar of discharging weaponry. The counter-attack had begun, although it was not quite what anyone expected. Not only were the trees flying, but they were moving along the ground of their own volition, using their ferocious branches to hit and tear and pull at the enemy.

'Fiberoids?' said Stash. A sly smile split his lips. 'The mountains here are full of trees,' he told the lizard.

'Shrtsk!' squeaked the farmer, and he loped off towards the sorting machine, leaving Stash and Quay alone.

It seemed to Stash and Quay that flying sequoias were not the most unusual thing they had seen that day, although it was a toss-up which danger to fear the most.

'Who knew redwoods could fly?' said Stash. 'Or were so pissed off.'

'So much for the job,' said Quay, watching the lizard creatures retreat into their ships.

'Yeah,' said Stash.

They paused to watch two pine trees eagerly dismembering a few Scintar soldiers.

'You know, Sid was right, these things do make a popping sound,' said one of the pines. It strode to Stash and held him up by one foot. 'Are we supposed to kill these as well?'

'Negative!' said a passing oak.

The pine laid Stash gently on the ground.

'The trees talk?' Stash said, righting himself.

Quay helped him to his feet. 'And walk and kill.'

'And fly, too.'

'Well, why wouldn't they?'

Stash pulled out his Star Gazer Tribune. 'Anything in here about trees being ancient warrior protector things?'

Quay bent his knee, grimacing. 'Nope, but I don't think the Scintar are likely to be interested in farming here anymore.'

'Look,' said Stash, shoving the front page into Quay's face. 'Only 137 subscribers now. Bad day for Star Gazer readers.'

'Well,' said Quay. 'Even if the Scintar leave, this world's all broken now. I mean, it never really worked for us anyway, but still. Reality isn't what it used to be.'

'Shattered,' agreed Stash.

'Way shattered,' said Quay.

As the fight raged around them, a row of purple paisley assault helicopters landed just a few feet away. Quay shielded his eyes from the swirling dust and thumping blades. The hatch of the largest craft opened and out oozed the biggest slug they had ever seen, in full combat fatigues.

'That is a seriously ugly chopper,' said Stash.

The beast slimed towards the boys as though they were schoolmates. 'Hello, gentlemen,' it said. 'I am Halbronson. Call me Hal.'

'Excuse me,' said Quay, 'But aren't you a…um…a…'

'Slug?' said Stash.

'A very large…'

'…talking…'

'…muscular…'

'…slug?'

'Better than the blue lizards though, doncha think?' said Quay.

'Brave words!' said Hal. 'But fear, my good men, is just nature's way of warning you that things are about to change.'

'So,' said Quay. 'Are you some sort of invertebrate truth sayer filter thing?'

'I don't think he's with the Scintar at all,' said Stash.

'You mean we're being invaded again? Before the first invasion is over?'

'I don't think invasion is the right word,' said Stash. 'I think Hal is more of a business-slug?'

Hal scrunched his face into what might almost pass for a smile, a Mona Lisa smile, but a smile none-the-less. 'Perhaps,' he said, 'you two have promise. Come with me.'

'Again? Listen, Mr. Slug Bronson,' said Quay. 'What if we don't want to go?'

Hal's face did that scrunching thing again but this time there was no mistaking his malice. 'I won't force you, but you don't really have many options,' he said, winking at them and cocking his head toward the Scintar sorting machines. 'You can take what I'm offering, or you can wait for the next farmer to come along. And they *will* come.'

Quay and Stash gave each other a knowing look. They had been Star Gazer Tribune readers for a long time. They knew.

'He's right, dude,' said Quay.

'Of course he's right,' whispered Stash. 'And even if he weren't, I make it a rule never to disagree with eight-hundred-and-fifty-pound garden pests.'

'Nine and a quarter, at least,' said Quay.

Hal nodded his approval. 'You have promise indeed,' he smiled. 'So, what are your names?'

'Horatio Vladimir Von Stuben de Quarter,' said Quay.

'I hate long names,' said Hal. 'And you?'

'Steve Ash,' answered Stash. 'Call me Stash.'

'So,' said Quay. 'We're new at this galactic farming game. Will we be working for you?'

'Oh no,' said Hal. 'I'll broker you two out to the government with the best deal, both monetary and otherwise.'

'We are not your property,' they shouted in unison.

'Think of me as your agent,' smiled Hal.

'That works,' said Quay, shrugging.

'I'm good,' agreed Stash.

'Excellent! Now, do either of you have significant others that we need to find before we go?'

Stash regarded Quay. 'Our girlfriends are in, like, Tahoe for the week.'

'Shall we fetch them then? Space can be a very lonely place. I fear our maidens are unlikely to find your…um…type especially attractive. You might be strapped for appropriate companionship.'

'Our girlfriends can come with?' said Quay.

The answer never came. A series of thundering explosions rocked the very fabric around them. Apparently, the trees were still at it.

'Give it up, dudes,' said Stash sadly.

'Yeah,' said Quay. 'You're just smashing the place up. What will be will be.'

'Man, that's deep.' Stash shook his head admiringly.

The slug glanced skywards and spun around, surprisingly agile for his size. 'Inside, quick,' he said, oozing back towards his chopper.

Stash and Quay raced after him. The hatch had barely closed before the ground splashed with falling shrapnel.

Rising Tide

Louise Cole

I SLID THE CAR INTO the only vacant space I could see, sucking my stomach in as I eased the Merc between a white van and a shiny blue BMW.

'Be careful opening your door,' I murmured as we shimmied from our seats. My daughter–twenty-five years younger and about twenty pounds lighter–waited for me by the boot. I clicked the locks shut and polished the neighbouring BMW with my trousers as I wriggled towards her.

'Okay?' I asked. 'We don't need to do this, you know.'

She turned her brown eyes to me... so like her father's. 'Of course I need to do this.' She fixed her gaze on the doors. 'You can wait outside if you want.'

'Of course not. It'll be good.' I smiled, forcing my eyes to crease.

'Just don't fight.'

'No one is going to fight. It's a visit.'

We swung through the buzzed-open doors and followed the warden, Melinda, up two flights of stairs.

'He's doing really well,' said Melinda. 'Settling in beautifully. I'm in my office if you need anything.'

I gave her a grateful smile and tugged at my jacket. I wished I'd had time to change when I left chambers. My suit felt like an unspoken reproach.

Dave leapt out of his chair when we entered. 'Carmel,' he cried, gathering our daughter into his arms. 'It's so good to see you.' He looked around him and opened his arms. 'Did I tell you I moved?'

'Yes, Dad, we know. We've come to see your new place.' Carmel held his hand as she perched on the arm of a chair. 'It's great.'

I watched her unfaltering smile, her hands gently grasping his as he sank back in his chair, and my heart bruised itself against my ribs, hot and swollen.

'Samantha.'

I forced a smile as Dave reached for my hands and pulled me down towards him.

'You look fantastic,' he said. 'Give me a kiss.'

For an awful second I was on a collision course with his mouth and I forced my head to the side so his lips glanced off my cheek.

He gave a small laugh. 'Typical Samantha. Always on your own terms.'

I pulled back. 'Nice place.'

'Yes. Did I tell you I've moved in here? It's not bad is it?' He shook his head. 'Not like being at home though.'

'Not yet. But it will be. This is going to be good.' I resisted the urge to pat his hand like I was reassuring a dog. I had promised us both I would never patronise him.

'I should have moved in with you. When you moved to that place in Hampstead. You told me to come and I should have listened,' Dave said.

Out of the corner of my eye I saw Carmel bite her lip. I took a breath. 'But you still had your own place when we moved to Hampstead. And now you have this.'

I tried not to breathe in the institutional smell, chemicals overlaying the stench of old meat.

'Oh, I have gifts.' Dave jumped up and rifled through a drawer. 'Where is the damn thing?' He bent over the drawer as though the effort had exhausted him and gave a hollow laugh. 'I thought being unemployed would be boring but it turns out you spend more than half your day playing hunt the keys.'

'Is this it?' Carmel drew out a slim box, wrapped in a paper bag.

'Oh, well done. There. That's for you.' Dave handed me the parcel as proud as a school boy.

I peered inside and drew out Continental chocolates.

'Thank you Dave, that's really thoughtful.' My hand caught fabric at the bottom. 'Oh, is this for someone else? One of your friend's kids?' I drew out the small Barbie Rocks t-shirt and checked the label. Age four.

'Oh no,' he said, gleefully. 'That's for Carmel. I remember you love pink.'

Even before I could think of a response, Carmel had snatched it away. 'This is perfect, Dad. It reminds me of all the great times we had when I was small.'

Her father beamed and I looked down, humbled.

Dave took his seat. 'So how's work?'

I stiffened. 'It's good. I'm busy.'

'Still making a fortune I bet. Good for you, girl. You always were hard-nosed enough to make a success of yourself.'

'I think hard working's the word you're looking for,' I snapped.

My daughter bounded up like a startled rabbit. 'Who wants a cup of tea then?'

People always compliment me on Carmel, her maturity, her grace, and I cringe with shame. Not because they are wrong but because it takes really twisted parents to turn a bright, normal little girl into such a diplomat.

'Oh, you've no milk. No worries, I'll go down and get some.' She flashed smiles like Morse code at us both–*Don't panic, I'll be right back*– and flitted out the door.

'She's remarkable.'

'She is.'

'You've done a good job, Sam.' He looked at me appraisingly. 'I knew I'd chosen well. You've not done bad at all.'

I gritted my teeth. Only Dave could be narcissistic enough to turn my parenting to his credit. I lose out both ways, I thought. After all, I make his failures about my poor choices.

'I know I was useless to you,' he said. 'I know I wasn't everything I should have been.'

I looked at the floor. What could I say? 'You're killing me with understatement'? Instead I replied, 'It doesn't matter now. It was a long time ago.'

'But I do know,' he said. 'I remember sometimes and it seems important. That I know. I'm different now.'

I managed a tight smile. 'Good. Carmel's doing well at school.'

He grinned. 'She's smart like her mother. I was thinking the other day about what a jerk I was when she was young. You would turn the living room into a stage or a carousel and I would just yell about the mess.' He paused. 'I am sorry.'

I opened my mouth to reply but he ploughed on. 'I missed out on so much. I could have enjoyed playing with you guys but I couldn't see it.'

My voice was like acid. 'You were hung over. I think pretending the room was spinning would have been a little redundant.' I sliced my nail into my palm. Don't fight. You promised. I sucked in a mouthful of warm, stale air. 'Mind if I open a window?'

I leaned against the frame. I could see my Mercedes soft-top in the car park below. I hated the sight of it. I had worked for what I had, worked damn hard. He had given me nothing. So why should I feel guilty now that we had a good life and he was stuck here?

'Where's Carmel?' he asked. 'Does she know that I've moved?'

'She's just making tea,' I replied. 'She knows. She's happy for you.'

Salt stung my eyes and my vision blurred. A photo swam on the windowsill and I grabbed it like a lifebelt. I showed it to Dave. 'Remember this?'

'That's why I keep it. There are some things you don't ever want to forget.' He ran his finger down the frame.

'Venice was spectacular. Even though they had the worst autumn storm in years.'

'Surf in the Grand Canal, all those trees uprooted on the Lido. We always did have a flair for the dramatic.' He smiled. 'That's not why I keep it though. It's because Carmel came out of that holiday.'

'I remember.'

'Bloody Venice though. Whole place was sinking. Streets just slipping into the canals.'

'You were drunk the entire time. You said it was like the streets were sliding away.'

'Really?' He raised an eyebrow. 'I was fun though, right?'

'Sometimes.' I kept my eyes on the image of the two lovers sitting on the steps of the Rialto. They looked so young.

'Thank you.' His hand closed over mine. 'For organising this for me. I know you got me the flat.'

I shrugged. 'Carmel worries about you.'

'She's a good kid. You did well.'

We sat in silence for a moment. I studied the eyes of the girl in the photo, trying to remember how she felt. I failed.

'I have dementia, you know,' said Dave. 'They said it wasn't the alcohol. Just one of those things.'

'I know,' I replied. 'I was there.'

'Of course you were. You were with me.' He dropped my hand, turned away in his chair. 'Do you think when I... when I forget you, do you think I'll understand? Do you think I'll know what's gone?'

I shook my head. 'I don't know. The doctor said you'll still be you, though. You're the same person, Dave, just with bits that don't work as well.'

'The same person.' He gave a hollow laugh. 'A mean drunken son of a bitch. That's an illness too, you know.'

'You don't drink any more.'

He wiped his eyes. 'I should never have lost you. I've always loved you.'

I swallowed hard, hypocrisy lodged in my throat like a rock. I clenched my teeth and my nails worked their stigmata around the leather strap of my handbag.

'You don't know what it's like. The compulsion. The forgetting.'

'I know what it's like to live with it.'

Dave turned in his seat, hands flat on the arms, like a judge. 'Sometimes you sound like you've never forgiven me.'

'We don't all have the luxury of forgetting.' I put my head in my hands, the sound of waves in my ears, like the waters of Venice still rising around me. 'I'm sorry. I shouldn't have said that.'

'Say what you like. I'm not the same person.'

I leaned my head against the cold window once more. The Mercedes looked like a hole in the fence, an unguarded door.

'When I forget, when I—'

I heard Carmel's voice in the hall, chatting to Melinda. I straightened up, to keep my head above the water line. I could see my daughter now, outlined in the doorway.

I couldn't leave if I wanted to. She would always be standing in the doorway. Needing me. Needing me to make it right. I moved to his side.

'We'll be here,' I said, squeezing his hand. 'We'll remind you.'

He wiped a tear off his cheek. 'Why would you do that? After everything?'

I sought for something like the truth, caught a tendril as it floated past. 'We stopped being married a long time ago. But we'll never stop being family.'

'So what have I missed? What are you guys talking about?' Carmel put the milk on the table.

'All about you, baby,' said her father. 'It was all about you.'

THE MORTICIAN AND MR GRIMLEY

GAIUS COFFEY

I HELPED MR GRIMLEY TO HIS FEET and together we stared at the empty gurney on which I had laid out his dead brother the previous night. It was some seconds before I realised it was down to me to break the awkward silence.

'He was there yesterday.'

Mr Grimley nodded, his tortoise-like eyes receding beneath deeply wrinkled lids. 'Are you sure this is…?'

The question hung in the air like an accusation, but we were a small outfit with space for only six and the mild autumn weather was still keeping people away. Discounting the insult to my professional pride, there was no possibility of an error as the elder Mr Grimley represented our entire business for the previous three weeks.

'It's definitely the correct gurney, Mr Grimley.'

His grief appeared to battle something that was altogether more complex and, in horror, I remembered the last clause of our agreement.

'He can't have gone far,' I said and recognised in my voice the same desperation that I had heard from countless customers, the same refusal to accept loss, the same anger, the same disbelief.

My wife had been pregnant with our first child when, over a decade ago, I met the younger Mr Grimley. Any doubts I may have had about his precise terms were silenced by the unusually large advance and thoughts of the home it would enable me to secure for my family.

Yet, even now, I found it incredible that the 'inability to bury' clause might apply. There were rumours about the mysterious disappearance of seventy kilos of Mrs Whitstanley's rockery on the day of her husband's memorial, but that was with the crowd down the road. Things like this did not happen to professional undertakers, and I considered myself one of the best.

Mr Grimley steadied himself with one hand against the empty gurney. 'You have disappointed me,' he said. There was nothing more to say.

'Frank!' I heard a sonorous voice behind me.

'George!' Mr Grimley turned, as did I, to see the imposing figure of his brother somehow managing to look dignified despite wearing just a split blue robe and a brown paper tag on his right big toe. The younger Mr Grimley smiled so that even the deep creases on his forehead seemed to turn up at the corners. 'You're looking… surprisingly… well.'

'Didn't I tell you?'

'You told me lots of things.' There was an edge to the younger Mr Grimley's voice, a resentful edge.

'You aren't still going on about that! Our wager was as clearly agreed as this one and I followed the rules to the letter, it's not my fault if you didn't think them through.' George marched over to embrace his brother affectionately. He turned to me. 'I don't suppose you know where my suit is?'

It was a somewhat irregular but reasonable request. I nodded and went through to the office where a perverse masochism masquerading as hope made me check the Grimley file. The specificity of Mr Grimley's terms began to make sense as I deciphered the complex wording of the punitive 'inability to bury' clause and realised I was liable for a multiple of the original advance. I didn't need to calculate the effect of ten years of compound interest to know that I was ruined.

They were deep in conversation when I returned with the suit, and George began to dress without pausing, barely acknowledging my efforts.

'…you see, I was right. The elixir of eternal life has a simple formula and you have lost our little bet.' George paused for a triumphal smile. 'You owe me five hundred thousand pounds.'

'I don't think so,' the younger Mr Grimley answered with a mischievous glint in his wizened eyes. 'My definition of immortality doesn't allow for,' he paused, looking around the mortuary with evident distaste, 'a gap in service.'

'Really?' George's voice changed; no longer warm, it was sharp, almost threatening. 'So I presume you have come up with your own formula?'

The younger Mr Grimley's eyes narrowed and the two distinguished old men, both now wearing identical pin-stripe suits, squared off against each other like boys in a playground. Their eyes locked, their rivalry marked by cold aggression, the type from which a man might act.

'You owe me five hundred thousand pounds,' George repeated.

'Or what?' The younger Mr Grimley reached for a small statue of an angel. It was one I kept in the viewing room to add a certain ambience that my customers seemed to appreciate, but it was also cast from solid-brass and its elegant wings, in the right hands and with the wrong intent, would serve as deadly weapons; a fact that was clearly apparent to both the Mr Grimleys.

It shames me to admit that I would've allowed the fight to proceed, hoping that the younger Grimley's malice would be enough to best his recently deceased, unarmed brother, and that the troublesome last clause might not be enacted. After all, where was the crime in allowing a dead man to die again? Surely the law is only concerned with the manner of a man's first death?

The elder Mr Grimley scanned the room, then reached for a large, porcelain urn. Decorated in an exquisite floral design with hand-painted gold lettering, it was the most expensive urn in the range and the embodiment of respectful remembrance. Though many of my customers could not afford this particular model, one sight of it was often enough to inspire them to purchase the cheaper next model down. It was also easy to grasp in both hands so that a tall man, like the elder Mr Grimley, could wield it as a club.

The elder Mr Grimley smiled. 'Mortal or immortal, Frank? Your choice.'

'You'll get your money,' the younger Mr Grimley said. He turned to me. 'I believe I'm due a refund.'

George and his brother looked at me, united by fraternal hatred of a profession they had good reason to despise now that they could dispense with it.

'I haven't got it,' I said. 'Take my business, my house. That's all there is. I could work for two hundred years and still not have the money.'

George smiled. It was not a nice smile. 'An instalment plan will do nicely.'

He retrieved a small bottle from his jacket pocket. 'Perhaps you would be kind enough to fetch two cups. One for my brother, and one... for... you.'

My wife has never understood why I keep working, nor why we could never afford a holiday when the business has grown so much in forty-three years. I wish I'd had the courage to tell her, but I was ashamed before, and now it is too late.

I'm going to miss her.

Underworld

C. M. Salter

THEY CALL TO EACH OTHER. Their voices fill the air with animal growls and grunts. I shiver, remembering last time. They'd found me bleeding but empty, confused. I can't let them find me again. I don't have the energy to defeat them a second time. My shoulder aches and my head still throbs where I fell down through the tree.

Head down, arms pumping like a world-class sprinter, throat on fire, gulping acrid air, I race barefoot across the gravel. Ignoring the sharp stones cutting into the soles of my feet, I cross the derelict open space, heading towards the remains of an ancient housing estate.

I reach the nearest wall and follow the decaying brickwork to its end. Turning the corner I find a large terraced area where, aeons past, scented flowers grew. I stop to rest, licking my cracked lips with a dry tongue. There's no saliva left to moisten them or ease my burning throat.

I cough, even that sounds hoarse and dry, no phlegm to shift. The bricks move behind me. Centuries-old mortar crumbles to sand, dusting the ground and my clothes. I move away. The houses aren't homes, just shells infested with weeds and rats. Nothing left where people lived and loved.

Behind me the barks change to baying, louder now in the empty wasteland. The hounds have either followed my scent or... I glance down at the blood on my cut feet. I need to hide and fast. I can't climb back into the safety of open sky. I scan the area for an escape, somewhere black. The hounds are afraid of places where demons dwell. They might hesitate, call off the hunt.

I might not remember who I am but I know this world, its denizens, both good and evil.

A flight of steps built into the terrace leads enticingly up into darkness. I race towards it, flying up two steps at a time. Catching my right big toe on the topmost edge, I sprawl head first. I spread my hands wide to lessen the impact. Gravel digs into my hands and knees, friction burns my chin.

But there's my salvation. Past a pile of building rubble, a long concrete slope leads down into the bowels of the earth. It looks like an underground car park. I pray I'm right. Maybe the unthinkable, a working vehicle. Anything's better than staying exposed in the light. My pursuers aren't visible, but growling noises are close, behind the house walls.

I half limp down the wide slope into the darkness. My toe is throbbing and the imbedded grit stings in the cuts on my knees and palms.

Where the slope levels out, I stop and listen. The ramp is bathed in sunlight, sunlight I might have enjoyed in earlier days when the world still turned. There's no safety in the light anymore. It's always daylight on the surface now, dry and bright. The second dwarf sun climbs higher into the bleached white, cloudless sky.

I step over the threshold and move from daylight into shadow. Facing the dark, I give my eyes a moment to adjust before moving on. I breathe out, relaxing my tired shoulder muscles, easing the tension in my broken right wing.

I've never heard of hounds following anyone into the dark. I take a moment to survey my chosen place of refuge. I can make out tall, grey, square shapes. No smell of oil or diesel. No rusting metal boxes in neat rows. No painted white lines on the ground—not a car park. I mouth a swear word, afraid to speak aloud.

Two wide corridors disappear into the black, one on either side. At intervals are small rooms with high-arched doors, like hungry mouths. One closed door stands opposite me.

At the top of the slope, metal scrapes against concrete. Thinking the hunters have found me, despite their terror of dark places, my breath catches, my arms splay wide in childish reflex.

They haven't found me. Instead a massive concealed shutter emerges from a metal plate in the floor. I missed it; how could I miss that? I watch it rise to the ceiling, blocking the only exit. The sunlight contracts into a thin sliver of white fire, then it's gone. The hounds will have to find another way in if they're prepared to follow.

My stomach churns, threatening to dislodge the remains of my meal, while my pulse thunders in my ears. It isn't a question of hiding any more; I need to find another way out. Each route looks identical. I take a step forward. Something tingles on my skin like a spider walking over my face. An instinct…I am not alone.

The door opposite me opens. Standing inside the small room is a creature of my nightmares—a Hellfire Demon.

It's humanoid in shape, but that's where the similarity ends. Its body is covered in snake-like scales. Every joint displays a wicked spike. Its arms, muscle-bound and huge, end in razor-sharp talons. Judging by the shape of its claws, it feeds by tearing its victim to pieces.

My knees judder, my hands refuse to stay still. I wipe sweat off my top lip and forehead; more sticks to the fabric between my shoulder blades.

Its cruel face sneers at me like I'm beneath its contempt, a bacterial life-form in the presence of royalty. An overlarge, raw-edged mouth, dripping blood, sits lopsided below two flat nasal holes. Red eyes glower at me.

The obscene manifestation standing before me is naked in all its 'glory'. The demon laughs, a sensual, throaty sound, out of place inside that abomination of a mouth. Our eyes meet. His laugh tells me everything. He knows I've noticed his manhood and found my own phallus childlike by comparison.

'Welcome,' the demon says inside my head. It—he—doesn't mean it.

The mental violation makes me want to vomit. Sweat and urine run out of me. Several flight feathers tumble to the concrete. I'm unable to lift my feet an inch from the floor. A puddle appears around my feet.

What is a Hellfire Demon doing here, away from the Underworld?

I berate myself. So stupid. I've been trapped, herded like some gormless animal. It's come for me. Anger fights with my fear and loses. My shoulders slump in submission.

He revels in my discomfort, his grin widening, until it looks like his face will split.

The demon, tall by human standards, stalks out into the corridor where I stand trembling and wet. Once free from the confines of the room, he elongates his frame. His knees, hinged backwards like a bird, straighten, adding another two feet to his height.

He approaches me, his chest mere inches from my face. I can smell his putrefying body odour. He stinks like a donkey's week-old corpse rotting in the midday sun. I found one once, in another life, when the world still turned.

He breathes in deep through his nasal slits as if trying to inhale the essence of me. 'Ah! Fear!' he moans. A shudder of pleasure courses through his body.

His remark ringing in my head, he turns on his heel talons. The move screeches like a fork across a bone china plate. He lurches off down the corridor, his talon spurs tap-tapping on the concrete, like some kind of bizarre Morse code.

'Come!' he mind-calls.

I bite down hard on my lower lip, a pathetic attempt to stop me from wailing in terror. I refuse to move; only bad things will happen from here. When I fail to respond willingly, he orders me.

'Come!'

My feet move, answering his command. I scream inside my head, begging my body to stop following him. I plead for it to turn around, to run in the other direction, away from here. Ignoring my pleas, my traitorous body follows the demon into the dark.

I don't know how long we walk down the corridor. My mind tries to unravel the confusing situation but I can't think, can't focus. Noises intrude on my thoughts. My ears pick up sounds from the closed doors further down. Some are low aching moans, others whimpers like a puppy waiting to be whipped for soiling the mat.

I try wiping the sounds from my mind; I fail. They creep along behind me as I, in turn, trail behind the demon, who glows a dirty, luminous green and smells like a cadaver.

The demon swings his head around to regard me, like a hawk scrutinizing its kill before it eats. He seems to sense my discomfort because he smiles, blood dripping from the raw flesh around his mouth. He says nothing.

After some time we arrive at a large open space—the car park I wished for earlier. At first glance it seems normal enough: stone pillars rise at regular intervals supporting the ceiling, areas are sectioned off into smaller squares with painted lines.

Lengths of heavy, grey chain encircle every pillar. I can make out human shapes ensnared within each chain. Bulging, panic-stricken eyes follow my movements.

A long rasping noise comes from one of the pillars. Thinking it's one of the prisoners trying to speak, I glance towards it. The chains move of their own accord—alive—some sort of reptile. The lengths of chain on another pillar rustle and tighten, accompanied by the sound of crushing bones; blood seeps between the links. The tiny amount of urine left in my bladder trickles down the inside of my damp pants.

I reach out my left hand to steady myself, touching an unoccupied pillar in the process. Something thin, dusty and cold rushes over my hand, tugging at it, drawing away the life. I pull my hand away fast. I never want to feel that sensation again.

Keeping my eyes down, I avoid the pillars. Whatever happens, I'm not going to join those poor unfortunates.

'Don't worry,' the demon mind-calls without turning. 'We have other plans for you.' His voice erupts into a choking, coughing sound. At first I think he's struggling to breathe—maybe my chance to escape?—then I realise he's laughing.

Following my captor against my will, I travel on through the hall and beyond, my feet bloody and aching from the unaccustomed walking.

A vast black pit opens in front of us. It yawns like a gigantic maw. I drop to my knees. Bile rises into my mouth; I don't know whether to be sick or swallow it. I gasp, cough.

The sound, louder than I realise, attracts the demon's attention again. He turns to consider me.

I try to run, to go back. I will my body to listen to me. My hands clench, the tendons stand out on my forearms, the muscles flex in my neck but I'm held in thrall to his command. My legs won't move.

The demon comes close. He smiles, wrapping one repulsive arm around me in a parody of a lover's embrace. I scream. My damaged angelic wing burns at his touch. Together we fall into the Underworld.

A howl rings out, shadows creep round the rim above. My earlier pursuers gaze down, fangs out and long tongues lolling. They've found another way in, overcome their fear of the dark. Grinning, they launch themselves into the air behind us.

* * * *

I can't do anything about the hounds. The demon doesn't seem bothered by them or the pain of my contact. He seems to revel in it. We drop into the black abyss. Someone close by me screams. The scream continues until the screamer has no air left.

The cold, tugging sensation I felt in the hall returns. It's passing me, whisking upwards to the surface. The scream is mine, I realise; a primordial yell of terror. I remember the cold sensation, its meaning: a lost soul.

Souls of murderers, rapists and abusers, souls trapped in the Underworld. Frantic, like me, to escape this un-life. Another greets me. This time it slides over my body on its journey to freedom. It creeps like cold water from my foot to my shoulder, clinging like a smothering greasy stain. On my shoulder it lingers: dirty, smelling like sulphur.

It's lost in the rising thermals. Despite my disgust, I hope it makes it. I don't remember why, but forgiveness is important.

I watch the demon as we fall like Alice in Wonderland characters. He tastes the air with pleasure like a gourmet dining on a fine meal. His long-forked tongue slides in and out his gash of a mouth like a snake. Where his skin touches mine, where opposites collide, the flesh doesn't just burn; it boils. I can't believe that he can still hold on; how can he bear it? The agony is threatening to send me spiralling into unconsciousness. Then I realise: he's enjoying it. He feasts on our pain.

We stop falling. We don't land or smash into the stone floor. We hover slightly above it, feet first. There's no sudden decrease in acceleration; my body doesn't feel...anything. It's an anti-climax after such a long fall. I hoped for an instant and painless death. I feel cheated.

Until the hounds, who jumped in after us, hit the floor unfettered by the demon's touch. They are annihilated. It's hard to see any single piece of dog left in the large puddle of red pâté on the dirt. An odd bone, a hank of hair, a small piece of muscle attached to an oddly angled joint. The demon grins, reading my thoughts.

'You are funny.' He gurgles, his laugh sounding like someone suffocating. 'I am enjoying your company. Such a shame…' his voice trails off. Both of us know my demise is imminent. As he speaks, he releases his hold. I fall the last four feet, just missing the pâté, an undignified landing of tangled limbs and bruises.

The demon steps down like he's getting off a bus, elegant and regal despite his size and ungainly stance. I am a peasant in the presence of hellfire nobility.

'I like that,' he answers, plucking the thought from my head.

The invasion into my mind still makes me want to vomit; and it's becoming annoying. I think, *I hope you hear me, you disgusting abomination.'*

'Come,' he calls, his manner giving nothing away.

I move of my own volition. There's no need to coerce me, no chase required and nowhere to run. My right wing hangs crookedly down my back; no point in returning to the world. I'm resigned to my death in whatever form it takes. My spirit flies apart.

From that point, everything becomes an effort. My body sags, my head droops, chin touching chest. It's an effort to lift my feet, one after the other. The tears fall, silent and sad.

He leads. I follow. We pass through caverns where monstrosities frolic with each other or with victims: animals, humans, and species I don't recognise.

Summoning up energy from somewhere I stop in front of the demon. 'What dreadful death awaits me?' I ask, looking into his red eyes. 'Why bring me all this way? Killing me in the hall would have been less hassle for you.' But not quite so amusing, I realise. 'That's it!' I exclaim. 'I'm your entertainment. You need an audience, don't you?'

He ignores me.

I return to my morbid ramblings and miss the change in surroundings. Gone are the grotesque underlings. This is an orderly, clean, almost clinical setting, like a hospital. We pass rows of empty beds and rooms that look like operating theatres. The Underworld cares for its denizens? I thought the injured were destroyed or, at best, eaten.

The sound of misery and suffering reaches my ears. We approach more rooms, but these are filled with creatures of all shapes and sizes, crying out in despair. At first I can't figure out what's wrong. More operating theatres, but these are working flat out.

The demon stops. I'm not sure if it's for his benefit or mine. I see a creature strapped down on a table. One of its limbs is being hacked from its body. We watch as a masked demon re-attaches the severed limb to another part of its body. Its left arm is re-joined to its right thigh. It is awake and in agony throughout the procedure. The nearby beds hold new-built monstrosities. These creatures appear insane, drooling and shrieking, ripping at their hair, their skin.

My horror is absolute. I vomit, grasping the damp wall for support. The screams alone could spin one into madness. This is far worse than the creatures in the chains above. I'd rather be back there, anywhere but here.

'God, help me,' I call out. I don't expect a reply.

The Hellfire Demon beside me laps up the misery, theirs and mine. His skin glows and he appears to grow taller. He looks down at me. Reflected in his eyes, I am a puny specimen of life.

'Why?' I force the question out through vomit-coated teeth.

He gazes down at me, his face ecstatic, at odds with the horror around us. 'Because,' he replies, purring like a big cat.

His answer makes me angry. Furious. My life is over but such a vapid response makes my anger soar.

'Because? Because what?' I roar at him, 'Because they deserve it? Because there was a great need? Because it's Thursday?'

He doesn't answer. He turns, spurs scratching the dirt, and walks away. And I? I do nothing. Impotent, I follow, trying to shut out the screams receding behind us.

A door looms over us. I hadn't noticed it. The adrenaline from my futile anger spills over into my stomach and head making me nauseous again. The throbbing headache returns.

The door is high, taller than the demon. He knocks once and announces his name: 'Ragul.'

I didn't realise the demon had a name. He glances at me. The door opens on to a room the size of a football stadium. It is damp, smells of blood and ashes. A central dais rises up from the floor, a gigantic stone chair at its apex.

A taloned claw smacks into the side of my head, sending me reeling. I fall face down onto the floor. My hand comes away covered in blood from my left ear. I turn my head to see Ragul abasing himself on the floor next to me, his forehead rubbing in the dirt. The word 'stay' burns into my mind. I stay prostrate beside him. Craning my head round, I notice movement.

I had believed the Hellfire Demon Ragul to be the most terrifying sight imaginable. I was wrong. Ragul is a child in comparison to the colossal creature occupying the stone throne in front of us.

One gargantuan leg swung over the arm rest, it is eating a cow. A whole cow: hoofs, horns, hide the lot. Fully thirty feet tall, it towers over everything. But that isn't what takes my breath away. Stretched across the creature's back are wings, over a hundred wings, angels' wings—wings like mine.

Ragul stays as still as stone waiting for his lord to recognise him. The Demon Lord continues picking his way daintily through the cow carcass. When he is done he throws the remains over his shoulder, it lands a gory mess on the ground behind him. Moments later the ground at the rear of the dais trembles, the soil rises up and splits open devouring the last of the cow. I stare open-mouthed as the leg bones sink from view.

'Ah, Ragul,' the goliath roars, acknowledging our presence for the first time. 'Come!'

Ragul rises. I notice he stands stooped, not reaching his full height. Is this out of deference, I wonder? More likely he doesn't want to be perceived as a threat to his master. Ragul growls, shooting a warning glance in my direction. I curb my thoughts.

The beast on the throne either can't hear my thoughts or thinks them insignificant. He lifts a blood-coated talon the size of my leg, beckoning Ragul closer.

'What have you there, Ragul?' he asks, spitting out his words, his black drool full of cow guts and blood. Ragul shivers in fanatical delight, excited and terrified at being so near his god.

'A gift my lord.' The words fall humbly from his lips. He stretches back for me, lifts me bodily, turning me round like a doll.

The beast grins, clapping his claws together with glee, spraying us with blood. Ragul and I receive equal shares of his recent dinner. Cow's blood covers my white wings. I shudder uncontrollably.

'Where did you find him?' he asks, childish wonder in his eyes.

'He entered the upper levels to hide, my Lord,' says Ragul. Seeing his master's puzzled frown, he continues. 'He is broken.'

'Wonderful, Ragul, so clever.'

Ragul bows so low at his lord's praise that his chin grazes the ground.

The beast raises his arms wide. I notice that his stolen wings are stitched together like a cloak, some surgically inserted into his spine and upper arms. There are gaps. Only a few, but enough for me to know my fate.

It's my turn to shiver. A small moan escapes my lips; understanding dawns.

'Prepare it!' screams the Demon Lord.

'At once, my Lord Baliel.' Ragul bows low again. Our audience is over. Taking me by my wings, Ragul drags me across the earthen floor. My heels leave two parallel lines in the dirt.

* * * *

So this is it. I feel weirdly accepting. Shock perhaps. I am going to have my wings removed. The scene in the operating room returns to me. Only this time, a hideous creature isn't going to be disfigured. This time it will be me strapped down on the table. I'm the one that's going to be screaming as my wings are hacked from my shoulders—while I'm awake.

My wings, taken for some petty Demon Lord to wear like a fashion accessory.

Nor will I be the first. Every pair of wings adorning Baliel came from an angel. So many. How could that many angels disappear unnoticed? Something nags in my head. I can't place it. Like an autumn leaf, it gusts away out of reach.

Where are they now, the others? Will I end up like them? Probably. I resolve to find them, free them. Wings are an angel's life.

With my promise, a flash of memory returns. I remember the lightning strike. The pain as I fell through the branches of the huge oak. The sickening crack of my right wing snapping against a branch, then nothing. Until this moment, my mind has been an empty vessel. Now it contains one memory: the storm.

I touch the area on my head where the lightning burnt. How did I survive? Even angels don't usually survive lightning strikes.

Ragul is watching me, observing, as I sieve through my meagre thoughts.

'First, we mend your wing,' he says. 'Your memory we'll consider later.'

I almost laugh in his face. 'What's the bloody point of mending it before you rip them off?' I mutter. 'Mend it afterwards.'

'Won't work.'

'What won't work?' I ask, confused.

'Wings don't heal once we remove them. We have tried before, and failed. My Lord Baliel wants pairs of healthy wings.'

'What does he want them for? Does he think he can fly out of here?' I ask, raising my eyebrows in mock amazement.

Ragul smiles. 'Yes.'

* * * *

I'm left in a locked room. There are dozens of white feathers littering the floor; otherwise it's empty.

I thought I knew despair but it's nothing compared to what I feel about the doom awaiting me. I toy with the idea of escape or suicide, but Ragul can read my thoughts. I don't stand a chance.

They bring food and a bucket. The guard is immovable. Eyes hidden behind long, wolf-like hair, sharp teeth undoubtedly able to rip my face off. Ragul assures me I wouldn't die; my wings would still heal. I get the impression Ragul would rather I tried to escape, just to relieve his boredom. It's not as though looks count for much in the Underworld.

The next few weeks revolve around the guard bringing food and changing the bucket daily.

A human comes and sets my right wing. He gives me painkillers because, he says, pain slows recovery. He is stick-thin and pale, like a worm. I guess he's been here a very long time.

No difference between night and day. No change from the four walls surrounding me. Walls I inspect out of boredom. Stone: cold, solid, like the floor and ceiling. The door: wood and rusty metal. The guard: never changed. He lives beyond the door unspeaking, unmoved by my actions and behaviours. I scream, yell, sing and fart—nothing.

Ragul visits but never comes in. I guess he's sent to read my mind, to check I'm behaving, not contemplating suicide or escape. He finds both ideas in my mind. I am a prisoner on death row.

My wing heals; twingeing and aching, it knits together. The spindly man returns to review and later remove the splint. He tuts and shushes me. More time passes. Three meals of green lumps, then no more. I guess why. I'm going to die now.

The door opens and Ragul steps in, ducking his huge frame under the lintel. He is taller than I remember, stronger and if possible even more virile. He gurgles with laughter.

'Come,' he says.

I don't want to but I follow.

The throne room looks the same. Lord Baliel lazes in his chair, finishing the remains of another meal, so casual that I half expect him to ask about the weather. Possibly I'm becoming immune to terror.

The skinny man scuttles in through the massive door pushing a trolley towards me. The wheels squeak like a mouse being ironed. The top is covered in a green surgical cloth. My stomach rolls. I look up from the trolley into his matching green eyes—nothing. No sadness, no pity. Behind him, two huge Neolithic monstrosities, covered in muscles and caked in dry blood—not their own—enter the room.

'Begin,' screeches Baliel his impatience evident in his tone of voice. The word is unnecessary we all know why I'm here.

The guards come forward. They've done this before. My knees give way before they reach me. I sink to the ground sobbing. It's unbelievable, unthinkable. They can't do this! I'm alive, awake! Where is their mercy?

There is none. Baliel has no interest in mercy. Ragul feeds on pain, even if it threatens to kill him. He is smiling now. I can't even wish they'd go to hell.

I kneel, my head bowed in the dirt. The guards grab my arms and pull them out to the sides. Their grip is like the walls of my cell: solid as stone. The remains of my clothing, a hotchpotch of rags, are ripped from my back. I have no hope.

The knife, sharp as a scalpel, cuts deep, slicing and digging into my warm flesh. The surgeon speaks as he works. 'I am severing your

muscles and tendons. I will leave the nerves and blood vessels intact.'
He seems skilful and bizarrely polite.

All I possess is my voice. I scream and scream, till it gives up. My
body hangs between my gaolers' arms, my head sagging in sweaty
exhaustion.

The surgeon holds up his first trophy, my left wing. Grabbing a
needle and thread from the trolley, he approaches Baliel, who leaves
the dais.

Baliel sniffs at the amputated wing offered to him. Smiling, he faces
me and drops to his knees, as though we are twin penitents.

I lift my eyes, for some ungodly reason, to watch the hideous scene
playing in front of me. Black drool falls from Baliel's obscene mouth
into the dirt; his smile is innocent as a child's.

The surgeon, trembling, stitches my wing into place just above Baliel's
left elbow. Neither of them makes a sound. I stare at the procedure
dispassionately. Why am I not writhing around in agony I wonder?
Why am I not unconscious? What magic is intervening on my behalf?

Ragul. He is containing my pain, my blood loss.

'Not yet, little one,' he murmurs. 'Not yet.' The muscles on his neck
bulge with his effort and concentration.

I understand why the guards are holding me. Ragul can't control my
body, halt the pain *and* staunch the blood flow all at the same time. He
has his limitations after all.

The surgeon returns to me, his hands full of my blood. He avoids
my gaze, takes up his knife once more. Fresh tears fall as the angel I am
disappears forever beneath his honed blade.

The second wing is secured in place upon the back of Baliel and both
sites are dressed. Baliel returns to his throne, his pleasure evident by the
way he croons and smiles, praising Ragul, who bows humbly.

Surprisingly, my wounds are closed with the same neat stitches Baliel
received. The guards release me and leave the room unbidden.

I notice for the first time that Ragul is sweating and agitated. His
eyes are furtive, refusing to meet mine. I can't believe he's feeling guilty,
but that's what I sense.

The sudden roar is loud and loaded with fear. Baliel bounds from
his throne shrieking and squealing, like a pig covered in napalm. He

careers and staggers round the room, yelling and screaming, ripping at his skin, his hair, a Demon Lord possessed.

I catch the edge of a smile flicker over Ragul's lipless mouth. It's gone in an instant. Still his lord flings himself about the throne room. Ragul doesn't move. He doesn't lift one talon to assist his master. He waits. The surgeon waits. I wait.

My back itches, then it burns. I start screaming, a sound to parallel Baliel's. I look at Ragul. He's removed his protection. He is smiling widely, an unconcealed, delighted grin.

The amazement must show on my face despite the pain, because he laughs out loud, a delirious exalted laugh. On the other side of the room his master wails and moans, throwing his body this way and that like a deranged cat throwing a burning mouse.

'Bloody hell,' I mutter. My own pain is easing as Baliel's behaviour deteriorates.

'Yes,' Ragul replies, laughing harder. The spindly surgeon next to me is smiling too.

'Stay,' Ragul requests without any mind force.

We watch Baliel. No one lifts a finger to help him.

'It is not our way,' answers Ragul in reply to my unasked question. 'We do not tolerate mistakes—ever. Survival of the fittest is practised here. Is that not the animal way too?'

Baliel is rolling back and forth over the ground behind his throne. He rears up on his massive tree-trunk knees, his back to us. For the first time I see my wings. My wings are on fire, a flaming blue river of flame spreading out across the angel-wing cloak, engulfing it all in bright, cleansing fire till not one feather remains.

As the final feather turns to cinders, Lord Baliel falls face down. His legs twitch, then his arms. His body is dragged under the earth by whatever subterranean monstrosity ate the cow. In moments he is gone.

I stare in disbelief. Ragul strides to the throne, ascends the dais and sits laughing like he's heard a terrific joke.

The spindly surgeon, standing next to me during all this panic, removes his tunic as if it offends him. On his back are two round lumps. Even as I watch, the lumps bud and blossom into a pair of beautiful, white, feathery wings. Angel's wings. He smiles at me and bows graciously, his wings fanning out in regal splendour. I look round at Ragul who nods once in the surgeon's direction. Taking a deep breath, the angel takes to the air.

'Don't be long,' he whispers over his shoulder. He flies to an exit in the roof and disappears.

I sit down on the ground exhausted, amazed and sad.

'What are you waiting for?' Ragul calls from his throne. I look over at him sitting there like the chair was made for him.

'I can't leave,' I answer. 'I've no wings.'

'You still don't understand, do you?' He speaks like he's talking to a child. 'Why did Baliel die?' His eyes are bright with excitement.

'You set him on fire?' I hazard, running my fingers through the dry soil at my feet.

Ragul roars with laughter, holding his shaking belly.

'You, you set Baliel on fire. Or more specifically, your wings did.' He stares me straight in the face with his demonic red eyes. 'Rightfully, you should be Baliel's successor.'

He watches while I take in this information. 'Do you want to be the new Master?' he asks mildly, picking at something in his teeth with a talon.

I think about it. Think of all the horrors I've witnessed, all the diseased minds and bodies I've seen. I think of living in the dark forever and answer truthfully.

'No, I don't.'

'Good answer, because I'd have to kill you otherwise,' replies Ragul, chuckling.

'If, as you say, I killed Baliel, I want to know how I killed him,' I shout. 'And then I want to go home. You can keep this stinking lousy, disgusting place.'

Ragul laughs until tears run down his ugly face, until the throne he sits in quakes beneath him. Wiping his eyes, careful not to impale himself on his own spiked arm, he leans towards me like he's imparting a vital war secret.

'Who is the most powerful angel? Who can destroy demons with his touch? Who sits in the first choir of the heavenly host?'

'That's easy: Gabriel,' I reply without hesitation.

Ragul waits, his face wet with tears of laughter. I wait.

The penny drops like a lit match into the abyss. My memory returns, a lightning flash searing across my brain. As the light erupts inside my head, white feathery wings burst forth upon my back.

'Shabach!' I cry in triumph.

Far away, the rattle of a multitude of chains falling to stony ground reaches my ears. The air fills with sweet music, a host of angels ascending. Above us, the second sun shifts and dusk falls across this world for the first time in centuries.

My back doesn't hurt. My wings are whole and healed.

It feels strange thanking a demon. I do it anyway.

Ragul bows modestly in reply. 'May I ask one small favour?' he asks his face unreadable.

I'm wary. Ragul has been polite throughout my detention but he's pure evil. He's lied, cheated and arranged the killing of his own high lord. He sees the doubt in my eyes.

'Such a short message,' he hedges. 'To Peter, at the gate.'

It seems churlish not to agree. Peter is irreproachable. I nod my assent.

'Tell him, "thank you".' Then, almost as an afterthought, Ragul adds, 'Oh, and add, "excellent lightning strike".'

Following the path my brother took, I soar into the arms of Heaven, Ragul's gurgling laughter ringing in my ears.

I know what the message means. I will deliver it. I am Archangel Gabriel, Spirit of Revelation and Truth, Messenger to God.

WETBACK

PATRICK LeCLERC

I PULLED MY THREADBARE DENIM JACKET close around me against the chill of the night. Using it to scale the barbed wire-topped fence hadn't done much for the battered garment's appearance, but it got me one step closer to prosperity.

The fence was the only real obstacle on our side of the Rio Grande. The guards were less than enthusiastic. They knew our plight and sympathized, but they were government employees and would do their jobs to keep up relations with their neighbor.

When they were being watched.

Many of them smuggled their own families over, and most could be bribed to turn a blind eye to a border jumper by relatives on the other side, where jobs were there for the taking.

I had no wealthy relatives. I hadn't had a steady job since my discharge. The government couldn't even keep up the military now. I had only my instincts and training to rely on. That and my determination to make a new life.

I reached the banks of the river. Weak moonlight glinted on the surface.

This was it. Once I was across, I'd be in the land of milk and honey.

And increased security. The guards on their side were serious. They wanted to keep us interlopers out. As though they hadn't come from Europe and stolen the joint from the Indians in the first place.

Time enough for life's unfairness later. I crouched in the scrub and watched the far bank for movement. The moon was in its last quarter and clouds slid across the sky. A perfect night for this kind of work. I stripped off my clothes, stuffed them in a plastic trash bag, tied what I hoped was a secure knot and waited for the clouds to give me my chance.

The night's chill on my naked skin made me want to hurry, but I fought down the impulse. Speed means sound means detection.

As the silvery ribbon of river faded to black, I crept from my hiding place and slid into the water. I stifled a gasp as I felt the river's chill and lowered myself into the water without a ripple. I swam smoothly, not breaking the surface with my strokes, just with my head. The bag trailed behind on a length of twine, floating on the river. It was far enough from me to be dismissed as trash if anyone saw it. I made a low enough silhouette to pass for a small animal even if the moon did come back out. I'd chosen my crossing point where trees overhung the current, dappling the light on the water.

Damn, it was cold. I tried to remember just how long it took a man to freeze to death. Not long, but that was just the body complaining. I'd had worse. It was cold, but no worse than sleeping on the streets in the rain. And once I got across, I'd have dry clothes to put on.

I climbed up the bank and crawled into the brush, clenching my chattering teeth. So far, so good. I opened my bag and pulled out my clothes. Still dry. Even better. I dressed quietly and shivered for a while before moving on. When you're cold you move too fast, take too many chances. Better to wait until I felt warmer. I dug in my pocket and put a hard candy in my mouth. Give the body sugar to burn. Not many left, but this was the time to use a little of my store.

After a few minutes my shivering settled down and I felt ready to move. I wiggled my toes inside my battered sneakers to keep the circulation going, wishing vainly for a pair of decent hiking boots. My sneakers were starting to come apart, and the trek through the rocky, bramble-choked desert hadn't helped. Soon, I'd find work, and then I'd never be footsore again. I'd have a pair of boots for hiking, sneakers for running and even a pair of real leather shoes with a nice shine to wear when I went out on the town. I exulted in the fantasy of owning more than one pair of shoes.

Suddenly a bright light pierced the night off to my left. I dropped to a crouch and froze. A voice in heavily accented English cut through the air.

'Freeze, *Gringo!* Border patrol! Stop where you are!'

I heard running feet and crashing through the brush.

Fuck!

The Mexican border guards had to pick this night for a fucking roundup. I heard other American illegals trying to evade pursuit.

I backed further into the brush, crouched lower and waited.

No way was I going back to Arizona. Since California pretty much broke off and fell into the Pacific in 2052, the economy of the American Southwest was in a shambles. There was no work to be had. That's why I joined the Marines. It was three meals a day, and they said it would make me more attractive to employers.

After I got out, I was surprised to find that there was no work for a rifleman in Phoenix. I had no money to travel to the industrialized East coast, and they weren't happy about absorbing us Westerners anyway. Hell, we might as well head to Mexico.

Around the turn of the century, a lot of manufacturing jobs moved south to take advantage of cheap labor and lax or nonexistent regulations. After the disaster, Mexico's economy thrived while ours sank like a rock. East of the Mississippi held out, but the epicenter of the West's economy was just a playground for seals now.

I wasn't going to get caught. The Corps taught me how to evade pursuit and avoid capture. I'd just hide, sit tight and wait until the *Federales* rounded up the night's crop of *Yanquis* and slide out after they left. I rubbed handfuls of dirt over my cheeks and forehead and the few remaining white spots on my clothes to keep any reflection from giving me away. I backed further into the thorny scrub and set down to wait.

The gleam of flashlights bobbed drunkenly in the hands of running men. I heard crashing in the brush and sounds of struggle as border guards caught illegals. I felt bad for the ones who got nabbed, but that was the risk we faced. Most of the border patrol were pretty civil about it. A search and a bus ride home was all we usually faced.

Running footsteps approached my hiding spot. *Oh please, God, don't let them trip over me and ship me back.* I tensed to run if it came to that. I was younger and fitter than most of these well fed *Federales,* so maybe I could still escape.

I heard gasping sobs from a young woman who was fleeing, the last of her strength ebbing away. Pity tugged at my heart, but I held my ground. If I stayed free I could make enough money to bring my family over. If I was sent back, I'd have to start over. I didn't want to repeat the last three days.

A lumbering Border Patrol agent caught up with the woman, tackling her a few yards from me. I closed my eyes, expecting to hear him zip her hands in plastic cuffs and march her back to the waiting bus.

Like I said, a search and a bus ride home, all expenses paid, courtesy of the Republic of Mexico.

Not this time. I heard cloth tearing, pleading in English and muttered threats in Spanish.

I swore silently. There were always a few people who used their authority to take advantage of those without power. I hated that.

I hesitated for a second. I'm not proud of it, but I did.

Cursing beneath my breath, I glided out of my hide. The agent had the woman pinned to the ground, her shirt torn open. He knelt between her legs so she couldn't kick him. He held both her wrists with one hand and tore at her clothes with the other.

I took a quiet step behind him and kicked him in the kidney. He grunted and folded up. I kicked him in the face when he looked up at me. He flopped over, writhing in the dirt. I could have killed him, and wouldn't have lost a wink of sleep over it, but that isn't the kind of thing other officers forgive. I'd heard Mexican prisons were nicer than the filthy lockups back in the States, but I didn't really want to test that theory.

I took his gun and tossed it into the bushes so I wouldn't be tempted to use it. I looked to the young woman.

'Are you alright?'

She nodded, stifling a sob as she pulled her shirt closed.

I helped her to her feet. 'Then run!' I gave her a push into the darkness.

She took off. I jogged a few yards behind.

As I'd feared, the sounds of the scuffle brought more Mexican agents. One grabbed at the woman running ahead of me, but I blindsided him and sent him spinning away into the darkness. Another caught the back of my jacket, but I slipped out of it, leaving him with custody of a faded scrap of dungaree. One finally caught me by the shirt, pulling me up short. I twisted, yanking him off balance, and dropped him with a short, hard right.

WETBACK

There were too many. As I turned to run, somebody swung a nightstick across the back of my knees and I stumbled. I went down under a wave of bodies as about half the Mexican law enforcement community landed on me.

Rough hands pinned my arms and searched me—thank God I hadn't taken the first man's gun—then bound my hands with zip ties and heaved me to my feet. A man with sergeant's stripes and a black eye slugged me in the stomach.

I grunted, but took it in stride. I didn't feel any moral outrage against the guy, he was doing a frustrating job. And that eye looked like it hurt.

Over the years, I'd learned to take a beating. The goal is to get through it. You fight back when you have to, you run when you can. If you can't, you just think of something else and wait for it to end. Righteous indignation is a luxury some of us can't afford.

Before things had a chance to get too ugly, a land Cruiser pulled up in a cloud of dust and an imperious voice snapped an order in Spanish. The border guards stood straighter in the glaring headlights and assumed professionally blank expressions.

The *jefe* in the truck barked at the officers and drove off. They hustled me back to a crowd of other *Norte Americanos* unfortunate enough to be captured.

'You are lucky today, *amigo,*' said the man who held my arm. I didn't bother to argue. I could have twisted away and run, but there were too many of them nearby, my legs felt rubbery after the punch I took and my hands were tied.

And I thought I might have pissed them off enough that they'd put in the extra effort to find me.

As I stood, panting, in line with the others, the officer from the Land Cruiser walked over. His uniform was immaculate. He was tall and athletic, and wore an air of superiority that said his distant ancestor was a Duke. His family probably followed Cortez. If he were American, he'd be a descendent of the Jamestown settlers with a ring from West Point or Annapolis and a Virginia drawl.

Not my circle exactly, but he had saved me from a beating.

He glanced at my right arm where my shirt sleeve was torn away, revealing my Eagle Globe and Anchor tattoo.

'Marine?' he asked.

I nodded.

'I remember your Marines from my time in the Pan American forces in Panama. They were good soldiers.'

'Gracias,' I muttered.

'I am Capitan Ramirez. I apologize for what Constable Ortiz was about to do to the *fugitiva*. He will be disciplined. It is unfortunate for you that your act of bravery will cost you your chance of escape.'

I shrugged. He seemed decent enough.

'You have your duty,' I said.

'I am glad you understand.'

By now, the Border Patrol had rounded up most of the refugees and were herding us onto the waiting buses. I didn't see the young woman. Maybe she got away. I smiled at the thought.

Captain Ramirez was still nearby. I felt I had to say something. Let him know I didn't blame him. I remembered being a peacekeeper in Panama. It's tough to be hated for doing a job.

'We all do things we don't want to do,' I said.

He turned. His eyes were filled with the contempt that sparks revolutions; Marie Antoinette would have felt insecure in that gaze.

'I have no qualms about sending you *Yanquis* back where you belong. Ortiz acted unprofessionally. He is a *bandito* in the coat of a *Federale*. That is unacceptable. But you…'—he struggled and failed to find a suitably disparaging term, and instead expressed his disdain with the tone of his voice—'you *people* flood our cities, live on our streets, take our jobs and drive up our crime rates. Stay in your own damned country. Your President Polk stole much of it from us two hundred years ago, and now you want to come here? Soon you will want to teach English in our schools and build Protestant churches and tax hard-working *Mexicanos* to feed and clothe you. What will become of our culture then?'

He turned on his heel and walked away. 'Fix your own country.'

I shrugged as I was marched onto the bus. I wasn't surprised. My ancestors came to America as ragged refugees fleeing the Potato Famine. We weren't exactly welcomed then either, but we survived.

I'd try again, and I'd succeed. This attempt cost me a bag full of clothes and my jacket, but I'd try again. And then, when I made it to Mexico City, where the streets were paved in gold and jobs were available for the asking, I'd bring my family south.

And we would thrive. Hard and lean from life in the impoverished American Southwest, we would flourish in the rich economic soil of Mexico, and all of Capitan Ramirez's arrogance wouldn't be able to stop it. Someday an Anglo Mexican will sit in the Presidential Palace.

Until next time, *amigo*.

Silver Cop

Janet Allison Brown

S EIKA WAS DOING THE PUPPY-EYES AGAIN. She was all short skirt and long locks. Most guys would give up booze for what her body language offered Mitsubi.

'Jeez, Seika, a little dignity,' murmured Casia, watching from the cover of the bus shelter.

Mitsubi wasn't interested anyway. He smiled carelessly at Seika and pulled a black helmet down over his spiky blonde hair. 'See ya, kid.' The huge bike between his leather-clad legs roared to life and he receded in a cloud of exhaust.

Show off, thought Casia. No one actually drove motorbikes these days. You rode them, but you sure as hell didn't try to control them. Mitsubi obviously thought he'd got his tamed. *Idiot.*

Seika stamped a foot in frustration, picked up her school bag and cursed aloud as a fat black raindrop splashed onto her face.

The public service announcement was instant and insistent. 'HEAD FOR SHELTER. HEAD FOR SHELTER.'

Globs of treacly rain oozed thick and fast out of the sky. The rain hadn't always been black, and thick, and indelible. Folk stories told of a time when rainfall was clear, without colour or odour. But as Casia's cyber-nannies always told her, water's black and them's the facts, akachan; the program that came up with stories about clear rain was obviously wired for humour.

Seika dodged under the canopy and shook her hair like a wet dog. 'Did you see him, Casia, did you? Goddamn this rain. It'll take at least three shampoo credits to get it out of my hair and I've only got one left until next month.'

'You can have one of mine,' said Casia.

'Did you see him, Casia? Mitsubi? He was on his bike.' She heaved a star-struck sigh.

'Of course he was.' Casia put two cigarettes between her heavily painted red lips, lit them and inhaled deeply before handing one to Seika.

'Thanks.' Seika took a deep drag and tried not to cough.

'So tell me about it,' said Casia.

'Oh I don't know. It's his hair. All spiky and—and gorgeous. And the bike. And the hair. What do you want to know? It's Mitsubi.'

'I know what he looks like,' said Casia, reaching under her regulation gymslip to hoick up her black stockings. 'Did he ask you out?'

Seika sighed again. 'Do you think I'm too young? Do you think that's the problem?'

Casia gave a husky laugh. 'Maybe you're just not his type.'

'Then what is his type?' said Seika. 'Look at me. Aren't I perfect?'

Casia gave Seika the once-over and then nodded her head towards the multitude of billboards flashing at them through the rain. 'Sure, you're a dead ringer for every jail-bait model on the planet. Maybe Mitsubi likes something a little different.'

Casia had no idea what Mitsubi liked. She'd been in love with him herself for as long as she could remember, and she'd never once seen him look at a girl. Not the gymslip bunnies, not the geisha-types, not the dregs—not even the very few originals, like herself. If Mitsubi had a type, Casia had yet to meet it.

Seika took a mirror from her satchel and surveyed herself critically. 'No,' she said at last. 'I'm perfect. Everyone wants perfect. It can't be my looks. But what else is there?'

'Good evening, ladies.' A Silver Cop slowed down as she approached them. She wore the new kind of skates on her iron feet, the kind that cut through the greasy puddles like a knife through flesh. The globules of rain beaded off her sleek, streamlined head: no worries there about shampoo credits.

'Almost curfew,' said the cop in a voice like honey. 'Do you require assistance?'

'No,' said Casia quickly.

'You have ten minutes until curfew,' smiled the cop.

Hell, thought Casia. *They've even got smile crinkles round their eyes these days.*

'In case you hadn't noticed, it's raining, dipshit,' said Seika.

Casia stepped on Seika's toe but the cop was already summoning one of Mr Dark's Original Rickshaws.

'Fuck,' said Seika, taking a step backwards.

'Please climb aboard,' said the cop. Her voice had risen a notch on the persuasion register. 'The driver will take you to your designated abode.'

The Dark driver's sickly white face grinned at them from inside the shadowy interior. There weren't many human drivers left on the roads. Everyone knew you couldn't trust a human behind the wheel—especially not one of Dark's sinister low-lifes.

'Take your eyes off me, baka yaro,' snapped Casia.

The driver's response faded beneath the roar of an approaching engine.

'Mitsubi!' squealed Seika, and the rain stopped, right on cue.

Mitsubi brought his bike to a halt. He lifted his helmet and his hair obediently sprang to attention. 'Is there a problem, officer?' he asked in a voice that could have melted metal.

'Buzz off,' growled the Dark driver. 'They're my fare!'

Mitsubi took a wad of travel credits from inside his leather jacket and handed a couple to the driver. 'That should cover it,' he said. His voice was friendly but his eyes said different.

The driver responded in angry Japican and manoeuvred his rickshaw back into the empty street.

Mitsubi lit up a cigarette. Taking his time. 'Can I give you ladies a ride?' he said at last. Even Casia, who had honed cynical to a rare precision, had to admire his arrogance.

'Five minutes until curfew,' intoned the Silver Cop. Oddly, her voice had notched right back down to pleasant. And she was staring at Mitsubi with a look very similar to Seika's.

What the fuck? thought Casia, raising an eyebrow.

'Hop aboard, girls,' invited Mitsubi.

'The last bus approaches,' said the cop.

'Yeah, but I'll get them home faster,' said Mitsubi.

Now both of Casia's eyebrows flew up; did he just wink?

'The last bus approaches,' insisted the cop.

'The faster you get these streets cleared, the faster you get off duty,' said Mitsubi pleasantly.

He had not looked directly at the cop. Not once.

The bus pulled over and the doors opened automatically.

'I'll take that ride,' said Seika eagerly, raising her skirt and flinging one leg over the back of Mitsubi's bike, making sure he got an eye-full of her thigh, naked above the stockings. She wound her arms around his waist and nestled her face into his back with a happy sigh.

'I'll take the bus,' said Casia.

'Both females should take the bus,' said the cop. She was unhappy now, this android with the wheeled feet and liquid-metal eyes. Regulations were regulations. Or maybe...

Casia stepped onto the bus and flashed her card at the automated driver. Then she sucked her breath in between her teeth as she caught sight of the searing look that passed between the sleek Silver Cop and the lean biker.

Casia took a seat and flicked a finger at the cop as Mitsubi revved the engine into life and spun the bike around. *So maybe he can tame the beast,* she thought. Seika wore an expression of pure ecstasy; in the light of new information, Casia didn't begrudge her the moment.

'Country View Or Sea View?' came a voice as the auto-screen scrolled across the window, obscuring the view.

'Give me back the goddamned glass,' snarled Casia.

'Country View Or Sea View?'

She sighed. 'Sea view.'

It was hard to believe they really weren't driving past an endless golden beach. Casia felt the day's tension begin to slip out of her; she grasped it back with an effort of will.

Technology ruled their laws, their lives...and now their love too? She pressed her forehead to the window, the sensation of cold glass defying the vision of a warm beach. *Now love too.* She breathed in, pulling all her hurt and anger to her. She wore it all the way home, like a cloak against the cold.

ABOUT THE CONTRIBUTORS

GARY BONN lives in Scotland with his family and an alarming number of accident-prone chickens. His writing is informed by his long experience working with children with social, behavioural or mental health difficulties and equally by his fascination with hunter-gatherer societies. He throws a mean spear. His novel, *Expect Civilian Casualties,* is published by Firedance Books.

* * * *

JANET ALLISON BROWN is the author of dozens of children's picture books and editor of several volumes of academic papers. She has written explorer guides, restaurant reviews, and articles on a range of subjects including traditional Arabic ship-building and handicrafts, adoption, education, faith and ancient cave paintings. Wife, mother, home-educator, writer and editor, she was educated at Balliol College, Oxford, and lives in rural Derbyshire. She likes stories, and makes them up all the time. Her novel, *The Walker's Daughter,* is published by Firedance Books.

* * * *

GAIUS COFFEY has had stories published by www.bewilderingstories.com, www.everydayfiction.com and the *Irish Times* newspaper and he is an occasional contributor to the *Flash Fiction Chronicles* blog with articles on writing and critique philosophy. One of his stories was shortlisted for the Fish One-page Story competition. He is currently working on his next novel while simultaneously trying to find a home for the previous one. He lives in Dublin with his wife, two cats and a beautiful little girl.

* * * *

LOUISE COLE is older than she behaves but younger than she looks. Over-educated and totally lacking in financial ambition, she has nevertheless managed to hold down various jobs in journalism and publishing. She finally forsook the lure of a regular paycheck to run her own media agency in North Yorkshire, thinking that quality time with her family and her writing would more than compensate for the lack of money. Yeah, well, you have to try these things. Louise contributes shorts to WriterLot. Her first novel, the YA paranormal thriller *The Devil's Poetry* will be out soon.

* * * *

Stepping away from the world of occupational psychology and small business consultancy, JAE ERWIN rackets around between writing, teaching yoga and exploring anything weird and wonderful that takes her fancy. She lives on the Pennines, has a husband, three sons, a dog, two cats and four vegetable beds – don't ask her which one she loves the most. Julie has two novels in progress, tentatively slotted into the magical realism genre, a scattering of short stories and somewhere in the dim and distant past lurk a poem or six.

* * * *

GIRDHARRY is in her fourth decade of life as we know it, and now lives an ordinary life with two children and one husband. She spent a great deal of her early years, restless, unhappy and searching for something-but-she-didn't-know-what and popping into the occasional therapy clinic or tai chi class on the way. In her wanderings, she discovered some fascinating aspects of life and it's these ideas which inspire her writing.

* * * *

STEVE GODDEN writes speculative fiction. He reads pretty much anything. He uses the second to fuel the first. (And writes this stuff in the third, because somebody told him once that he should and he didn't like to argue.) Other than that, Steve's just a bloke of independent penury and incidental personality. He also writes under the name T F Grant. Well, gotta have some variety in your life. His novella, *Tales of the Shonri: City of Lights,* is published by Firedance Books.

* * * *

A salesman for most of his adult life, ALF HAYWOOD has decided to brush off retirement in favour of being a full-time writer. He started writing romance and adventure stories about three years ago. Now his mission is to prove to his wife and family that all those hours huddled over a computer in his office were not wasted.

PATRICK LECLERC makes good use of his history degree by working as a paramedic for an ever-changing parade of ambulance companies in the Northern suburbs of Boston. When not writing he enjoys cooking, fencing and making witty, insightful remarks with career-limiting candor. His novel, *Out of Nowhere,* is published by Firedance Books.

* * * *

SHUNA MEADE lives on a tropical island in the Caribbean, with her husband. Paradise inspires her to write poetry and short stories for adults and children, several of which have been published online. She is a graduate of St Andrew's University in Scotland and has been a writer in hiding for as long as she can remember.

* * * *

Ex-millionaire and doctor of logic, CATH MURPHY is a freelance writer and co-host with Eve Harvey of Sluttylemon (www.sluttylemon. com), the world's only naked podcast. Three words can describe Cath: mature, irresponsible, contradictory, unreliable… oh wait, that's four…

* * * *

Born in Kent to working parents, C.M. SALTER was a typical latch-key kid. She fell in love with English in primary school and fell in love again at age 11 with sci-fi, courtesy of Isaac Asimov. She left school aged 15 and became a nurse; long shifts and lonely days. Carol is married with one son, cats and a Harley Davidson. She still reads fantasy and sci-fi, and wrote her first novel age 42. She has now written four and shows no signs of stopping.

* * * *

BILL SAUER is a former musician, former photographer, graphic designer by day, and aspiring writer by night and weekend. He has scribbled down millions of words since childhood. The words just come, and who are we to try and stop them? Husband, brother to a legion of siblings, doggie daddy to mutts and strays. Often mistaken for a big, dumb gorilla until proven otherwise, which is how Bill likes it. Then it's always a pleasant surprise when the truth is discovered: that boy can write, can't he? Especially when it's Bill doing the discovering.

REN WAROM is a writer of speculative oddities, not known for an ability to fit into boxes of any description. She's a certified Pirate-nun, mum to three spawn, slave to several cats, writing obsessive and general weirdo. The word *askance* was invented for the way people tend to look at her. For her sins, Ren is now represented by the fabulous Jennifer Udden of the Donald Maass Literary Agency. At some point, evidence of this union will land in a bookshop near you. It's recommended you buy hazard gear in preparation.

* * * *

WILLIAM WEBB JNR is an SFF—short, fat and fifty. He believes life's passion lies within absurdity, that Douglas Adams was a prophet, Pratchett is a genius, and Irma Bombeck died too soon. Along with a lifetime of experience as a CFO (not bad for someone with a marketing degree), he is also a writer for regional papers. His fiction is a rambunctious mix of sci-fi and humour.

ALSO AVAILABLE!

Available from Firedance Books...

THE WALKER'S DAUGHTER by Janet Allison Brown.

When her mother dies at the hands of a silver-haired figure in black, six-year-old spirit-walker Cora Bloux hides out in her own body. Twenty years later she's still there, fiercely maintaining an outwardly stable, conventional life.

But when her own daughter is hit by a car, Cora is forced to spirit-walk again—and discovers that the spirit world has been waiting for her.

In the extraordinary, fast-paced world of spirit-walkers, body-swappers, rock bands and second chances, Cora must discover her true self and learn the ordinary lessons of courage, trust and love.

To see the world as it really is, sometimes you have to close your eyes and... walk.

Also Available!

ALSO AVAILABLE!

Available from Firedance Books…

EXPECT CIVILIAN CASUALTIES by Gary Bonn.

Jason has spent the last six years living wild on beaches. Now he's seventeen and a feral girl walks into his life.

A girl with no name.

He calls her Anna. She's fun, she's kind—and she's the most dangerous person in the world.

The most unusual love story, and a truly strange war story… Expect Civilian Casualties turns how we see the world upside down.

Also Available!

Available from Firedance Books…

TALES OF THE SHONRI: CITY OF LIGHTS by Stephen Godden.

Darkness never falls in the City of Lights. The last hope of a broken world, the remaining Shonri warriors brave the ever-vigilant city to fight their war against the vicious Magi—or meet their deaths. For the last witch Medina, powerful, seductive, and untrustworthy, has sold her art to their enemies.

Can the handful of Shonri end the battle before Medina's magic reveals them? Can Medina survive her attempts to use the Magi for her own means? And can any of them live with the results of the battle they are about to face…

For while they scheme and fight, something stirs beneath the City of Lights… something more perilous than death itself…

Also Available!

Available from Firedance Books...

THE BEST OF WRITERLOT Volume One.

Wild women, warriors, the first moments of love... Muses, metafiction and murder. Find new voices, new series and cracking stories in this dizzying collection from the WriterLot team. WriterLot.net produces great new fiction for its followers every day. This collection celebrates some of the best, filled with unforgettable characters, heart-stopping action, and the trembling uncertainty of personal relationships. It captures the essence of what it is to be human (or, in one case, what it is to be a dog).